The Russian Spymaster's Legacy

Mark W. Doyle

ISBN: 9781081816186

DEDICATION

For my darling wife Kathy Diskin Doyle, surely one of the FBI's finest, and my beloved and beautiful family both sides of the pond; Doyle, Diskin, Galloway and Faure.

CONTENTS

ACKNOWLEDGMENTS

With special thanks to Kathy for her constant help and encouragement and to my editor, the "other" Cathy Doyle. And to my closest former US Law Enforcement and District Attorney friends, without whom there would be no book: Joe B., Brett and JoAnn.

1 THE BRIDGE

September 25

I couldn't see Kirilov or my quarry. Scanning again, the handsome Germanic looking and fashionably dressed twenty-something Kirilov caught my eye as he lingered by a double-parked blue Audi. He nodded in the direction of the River Moskva and following his cue I spotted the fat man I was looking for ambling along twenty yards ahead. Despite my rheumatic knees I doubted I would struggle to keep pace with Balenkov.

Having marked my target, his ample frame became easy to pick out among the sparse Muscovite pedestrians that evening. As I set off, I heard a car door slam and a reluctant engine splutter into life behind me. Balenkov passed two cuddling young lovers looking in a shop window, clinging to each other like survivors to a life raft in a storm. I doubted either would be saved by the other. The low late summer sunshine escaped the clouds, caught the shop window and illuminated my reflection, an unremarkable, overweight, middle-aged man with bad posture.

With my growing beer-gut I looked more like the much-missed KGB border guard I used to affectionately call 'Papa' than I care to remember.

Mikhail Balenkov, aged forty-seven, born St. Petersburg, qualified lawyer, property agent. That was as much as I could readily recall from the file Kirilov had thrust my way earlier that afternoon. It remained in the all too obviously effeminate 'man-bag' I was embarrassed to be carrying. 'Calvin Klein' the metal tag broadcast, to add to my discomfort and no doubt his amusement. The rumors spread in the FSB canteen were that Kirilov was gay, but I largely attributed this gossip to envy of his youth and good looks. He knew of the rumors and played up to them, mostly to annoy the old-fashioned former KGB types, like me. I have to agree that he had a point. My age and traditional approach had in recent years earned me the nickname "Yuri" at work after former KGB Chairman, and ultimate old-school bureaucrat, Yuri Vladimirovich Andropov. Kirilov lapped it up when he heard.

The Moskvoretsky Bridge seemed to be the direction in which Balenkov was headed. I texted Kirilov. The reply was instant:

Copy
Pass you and pull up on bridge

His English was as good as mine even though I had worked in England for a few years. FSB language training must be better than the seemingly endless KGB language classes I had taken all those years ago. Luckily not every Russian I was worried about could speak English well enough to follow our conversation in real time, should they be monitoring it, which seemed a real possibility.

Beyond Balenkov the Moskvoretsky Bridge and St Basil's Cathedral lay dead ahead, and the Kremlin loomed large to my left. Since I was a kid its enormous deep red walls had enchanted like some far-off romantic Alpine castle. As I got older the same edifices began to bully and intimidate me, like other Muscovites, with the half hidden golden topped buildings inside projecting not just power and majesty but also dark secrecy. The last of the Tsars and the Communists may have fallen but nothing had changed. Nothing would ever change in Moscow.

Now the Kremlin also loomed ever larger in my investigation. It could be the very reason I was now following Balenkov. He had come out of his apparent daydream and picked up his pace. A man with his physique must be sweating under the lingering sun. Even without it he would have been dripping knowing the FSB was after him. What he didn't know, but I now did, was that exactly who from the Russian Intelligence Services got to Balenkov first would determine if he lived or died.

My attention was grabbed by a motorcycle and its rider and pillion passenger, both entirely clad in black, slaloming noisily between the crawling traffic. I watched motionless as the passenger raised his arms level and fired the gun I now saw in his hands. There was no sound prior to the bystander's screams. A silencer. As my gaze turned back in the direction of my target, I saw Balenkov's now broken frame slumped to the ground. The motorcycle sped away, weaving between the Moscow traffic at suicidal speed and was gone in what seemed an instant.

I held out little hope that the police car that had happened to be on the bridge and was now in pursuit would get anywhere near catching the professional gunmen. The Russian Intelligence Services trained their own far too well to be caught by street cops.

My best lead in "the case" lay dead or dying, almost within touching distance of me. I knew fellow FSB or SVR officers were likely responsible for the shooting and this knowledge filled me with anger and revulsion.

An aging blue Audi screeched to a halt alongside me.

"Boss, get in."

Without answering I lowered myself carefully into the passenger seat, ignoring my protesting knees. We disappeared among the gleaming new imported cars making their way back to Moscow's more fashionable neighborhoods as the working day drew to a close.

Five cars behind the two plain clothes officers following us in an unmarked van were probably the only ones who noticed the battered saloon move off. A wailing ambulance and police cars drew attention towards the crowds now gathering around the body at a peculiar angle on the pavement. I sat there in quiet fury, struggling to stop my hands from shaking. My mind was racing. All thoughts added to the growing fear that was in danger of overwhelming me.

"U-turn now! Now!"

He floored the accelerator and veered across the front of an old taxi. Barreling across the central reservation he forced his way between startled drivers on the other side of the road causing one to glance a slower moving bus on its inside.

A chaotic mini-pileup ensued. The taxi Kirilov cut off

had slammed its breaks on. The suits in the minivan behind were alert and stopped in time, but the driver behind was focused on the scene around Balenkov. Distracted, he rammed the minivan into the back of the stationary taxi in front. The two trapped motionless men caught my eye. They seemed to be the only ones on the bridge not gesticulating at the lunatic in the blue car that had just caused mayhem.

"Well done. We've lost them."

"Them? Who?"

Ignoring his question, I ordered him to drive us back to the hotel.

In truth I didn't know the answer and I had no idea where to go. More frighteningly I was just trying to buy some time to think where we could even be safe. And with Balenkov dead, where were we with the case itself?

As Kirilov navigated the increasingly hostile traffic my thoughts turned back to the beginning in an effort to plan our next move and hopefully keep us out of the sights of assassins riding fast motorcycles a little longer. I redirected him to drive back toward the city center, in the opposite direction entirely. I didn't want to admit that I was not sure how safe we would be anywhere, even in the middle of Moscow, even in daylight. It was difficult to believe.

The case had started nearby, in Gorki Park, where just four days ago Moscow Prosecutor Yevgeny Litvanov had arranged a covert meeting with me. It had turned my world upside down. I had known it must be a serious matter for Litvanov to suggest meeting in a public place near to, but not in, one of our offices. Beforehand I had no clue just how serious.

I never warmed to him. I thought he was a vain and self-serving politician, although I did respect him for being a good prosecutor. Not one for small-talk, he had opened our meeting with an explanation that an envelope had been delivered to him by courier the previous Friday afternoon. It was from Markov, the top man in the Moscow coroner's office and someone I had come across more than once investigating the worst of the city's violent crimes over the years.

Litvanov explained that in the envelope was a note from Markov's wife. It said that her husband had left specific instructions for a sealed file to be delivered to the prosecutor personally in the event of his death, and she was complying with her late husband's wishes. She added that as per her husband's explicit instructions she had left the file sealed and was unaware of the nature of its contents, which were for Litvanov's attention and his attention alone.

"Double back and take a turn. Check your mirrors."

Litvanov told me that he opened the sealed file in the office after everyone else had left for the day. It contained a copy of the autopsy report for Colonel Filipp Mikhailovich Kislitsyn.

I remember interrupting him, quite angrily, but not exactly what I said. He had let me vent, then returned to telling his story.

The report was an original type written version and was labeled as a draft. It had been completed by Markov himself, and was signed with his usual unintelligible scrawl in the green ink he had always insisted on using. Attached with a paperclip was a poor-quality photocopy of the filed official report with the Moscow Coroner's stamp. The two reports were different. The published final report contained one small, but significant, omission. A single sentence had been removed which documented that traces of Polonium had been found in an analysis of Kislitsyn's hair.

It was too much. I had challenged Litvanov.

We all knew Kislitsyn smoked all his adult life and had died of cancer. Besides, he had served for years in the military and at times must have been in close proximity to our older nuclear weapons, most with dubious safety records.

But my objection had been made with a growing realization of the truth, albeit a reluctant one. Markov was no fool. The coroner's inquest had recorded that Kislitsyn had a brain tumor while at the same time recognizing he had developed lung cancer. The assumed cause of the cancer was now thrown into doubt by the traces of Polonium found.

"Left, take the bypass."

Polonium poisoning had become notorious after the murder of former Russian Intelligence Service officer Alexander Litvinenko in London in 2006. Years later, after Russia's annexation of Crimea, and when politics permitted, authorities in the United Kingdom had named officers of the SVR, the Russian external intelligence service, operating under Vladimir Putin's orders, as the assassins.

The implications of finding such a rare radioactive substance as Polonium connected to Kislitsyn's death were obvious and frightening, no doubt in Litvanov's mind necessitating the incognito meeting that day.

I confirmed his fears that if anyone was using Polonium to kill off people it had to be someone connected to the Russian Intelligence Services, more specifically someone within the old Department V of the First Chief Directorate of the KGB. Department V had been responsible for 'wet jobs' as state sanctioned assassinations were euphemistically known back in the day.

Some of these old KGB assassins had stayed on with the SVR. After a lull in the early post-Soviet times demand for their specialist services in Putin's Russian Federation has been on the increase.

Litvanov asked me to conduct an off-books investigation, with no record to be made in FSB systems and no vulnerable digital trail whatsoever to be left. To do otherwise would seal our fates. Only when our investigation was complete could we decide what to do with our findings and who we may be able to trust.

Despite our previously cool relationship he had told me how he knew I was the only man for the job. How could I not be? Kislitsyn had been not just my mentor and inspiration but also my best friend.

He asked me if there was an experienced colleague in the Moscow office of the FSB that I could rely on to assist me. There was not. All those I would have considered had retired or had been dismissed. General Valentin had assumed control and wanted the last of the old guard gone. The new bosses, Putin cronies to a man, just like Valentin, had put any who remained out to grass.

On the plus side I was working on a few minor corruption and extortion cases. My bosses couldn't care if

I filed reports on them or not, as long as I didn't bother them. It would be good cover for me to get out and about and do what I had to do.

I came up with the idea of finding a fresh-faced youth straight from the Academy, but already in someone's bad books. A clean skin that Valentin and the rest had not had time to get their claws into and someone they already didn't care for. In the following days I had identified a young handsome blond officer, fresh out of spy school, who had unsubstantiated "suspicions of homosexual tendencies" hanging over him.

As I recall, after the meeting I headed straight for the express bus home. I remember I had a strong feeling someone in the shadows of the park was keeping pace with me as I walked towards the bus stop. I was on edge. Stopping I asked some dropout walking by for a light despite the working lighter in my pocket.

Turning away from the wind to shield the flame I could scan the shadows. I had seen nobody. But spies as old as me somehow always knew when they were the hunted rather than the hunter. That night I knew. And knowing frightened me.

This time a nod in the direction of the main road was enough to redirect Kirilov.

In the silent car the fear was as tangible as the feeling I had back in the park. It brought me back to the present just like a particular taste or smell can transport you in an instant from one place and time to another.

As we joined the faster moving traffic, I processed my silent terror. A scared man, speeding away from a murder scene, with unknown pursuers. Fear had marked the start

9

of my investigation at the Litvanov meeting, had been present throughout and now marked what seemed to be the end of the road with the death of Balenkov right before my eyes. Now what? Kirilov slowed the Audi as we approached the turn light.

"Pull over and watch."

We sat in silence for several minutes letting the cars and busses go by, looking for other vehicles pulling out of the traffic and stopping. Glancing at the second driver's mirror, conveniently angled for front passenger use and fitted at my insistence to all our cars, I scanned my side of the road. Despite Kirilov's rookie status I was confident that his training was sufficient to let him take the other.

"Give me your phone."

After a moment's hesitation, having read my expression, he took his iPhone out of his jacket pocket and handed it over. With difficulty I took my ancient flip-phone from my trouser pocket and threw both in the glove compartment, slamming it shut.

"Have you got somewhere to go tonight? I don't think we should go home until we figure out who the goons in the van on the bridge were."

"Tanya's."

Kirilov's broad smile said it all.

"Girlfriend?"

"Could be."

"Leave the keys in it. With a bit of luck this old heap

will be towed or stolen and the phones will lead someone on a wild goose chase. Walk with me to the Metro. We can pick up a couple of burner phones, then we'll split."

We headed down a side road until we found a corner shop displaying a bright orange 'Skylink' logo. I paid cash for two of the cheapest models they had.

Swapping numbers, we left the store and headed for the nearest Metro station.

"Don't use this phone to call anyone else, not even Tanya."

"Got it boss."

"Get a good night's sleep. I'll call you in the morning after I've made a few calls tonight. Keep off the internet, even using Tanya's accounts."

"That bad?"

"We don't know how bad yet. Better safe than sorry."

"I know the drill. See you tomorrow."

I waited until Kirilov had descended the escalator to the Metro before I turned and headed for the bus stop. The younger ones can laugh at me for being "old school" but give me a bus over a subway train to lose a tail any day. You were trapped on a subway system with limited exit points. On a bus you could escape anywhere.

2 KISLITSYN

September 21

After my meeting in Gorki Park I stuck to busses to get back to my neighborhood. Alone with my thoughts and with the nagging suspicion of being followed I decided not to stay at home.

I had an army veteran friend living on the floor below me who kept a key on a chain you could reach through the letterbox. He was away visiting his son, who he was so proud to tell everyone was a diplomat in our Foreign Ministry serving in Germany. I knew that from his apartment I could look out for people watching mine, looking for me.

Mine was a run-down suburb that had in years gone by been the reserve of Communist Party members and security agency employees. As was my routine since Viktoriya had passed away, rather than go straight to an empty apartment I headed to the local street corner bar.

Three years already since she died. It seemed like yesterday.

The Kurant had seen better days. Chrome and bright red plastic high stools at the bar looking like they belonged in the seventies, as did the bearded flabby barman, who sported a stained white apron over his faded three button t-shirt and baggy jeans. He and I nodded to each other but neither of us spoke. We knew each other well enough not to bother.

He poured me a glass of imported lukewarm Pilsner and a vodka chaser, the usual for his most loyal and most antisocial customer. Not waiting for the vaguest confirmation, he put he put a slice of lime in the vodka. It was the closest I got to my "three a day". Viktoriya used to nag me to eat fruit, which she had read in one of her foreign magazines was the secret to a long life. I had always counted each lime in my vodka as one so I could answer her pointed questions less dishonestly. The habit had stuck.

I took up residence on my favorite stool at the end of the bar which had a poorly angled view of the TV, leaving the other customers some distance away as they huddled together to watch football or hockey or whatever. I liked being left alone with my drink and my thoughts. Tonight CSKA, the old Soviet Red Army team, was playing Dynamo, the old KGB team, in a big match. The other locals were glued to the game and did not take a second look at me. They were more than used to ignoring the local grouch.

That night I had chance to appreciate the other reasons I preferred my spot at the bar. It would have been the choice of any experienced spy who was good enough at his job to stay alive long enough to get to my age. With the end bar stool, I had my back against the dividing wall, was placed within a few steps of the rear exit and had the front entrance and street beyond in full view, even if the TV was not.

By the time I was half way through my first Pilsner, having downed the vodka in one, my mind had drifted back to my meeting with the prosecutor, slowly and methodically going over all we discussed earlier that day. I was trying to keep what seemed a tidal wave of questions and emotions at bay.

It was hard for me to think of Colonel Filipp Mikhailovich Kislitsyn without getting emotional. With my father away so often as a KGB border guard, which I long suspected is how he wanted it, my mother had brought me up almost by herself. I remembered a poor and often hungry childhood and a lonely one at that, as my mother had been unable to have more children after complications with my birth. Perhaps that's why she had doted on me so.

In those days the KGB was like a family business, often trusting the children of current or former officers before others when it came to choosing those to serve. Parents in the service also had a chance to offer inducements and call in favors to push their sons and daughters claims. The rewards and opportunities being in the KGB brought, particularly travel, the choice of state provided apartments and, most cherished of all, access to foreign goods, were too attractive for families to let go.

I was recruited into the KGB during my conscripted service, first as a grunt before I ended up in signals under a promising young technically minded sergeant named Kislitsyn. Then he was quickly mastering the new electronic cypher machines we had been equipped with. Unlike junior officers from the countryside Kislitsyn had at least seen something of the newer technologies.

He became a father figure to me. Back then I was a shy and introverted kid kept from seeing as much of life as I should have done by an overprotective mother. Soon after getting to know him, Kislitsyn's technical competence and steadfast Communist loyalty were rewarded with his promotion to Lieutenant. A transfer to Moscow and the First Chief Directorate of the KGB followed, a posting with the Counterintelligence Department. One of his first moves was to have me transferred. I was a quick learner and eager to please. He had taken me under his wing and we had worked together ever since.

I had always admired him as a leader and a patriot, although I did not view the Soviet "good old days" through the same rose-tinted spectacles he had worn. I had little time for politicians.

Like many Russians my disillusionment with the Communist leadership was complete with the use of Red Army troops to crush the freedom movements in neighboring Hungary and Czechoslovakia. In those days you had to be careful who you shared your political opinions with, but in Kislitsyn's company I had always been able to say what I thought. He may have been a diehard Communist but he was no fool and no snitch. He enjoyed an argument about politics as much as anyone, perhaps even a little too much for my liking.

Kislitsyn was never afraid to say what he thought to the bosses either, right up to the Directorate heads. He was unwavering in his opinions and not intimidated into silence like so many of his rank. Perhaps this is why, having risen through junior ranks quickly, his progress stalled. Later, as the Soviet Union collapsed following Gorbachev's 'Perestroika' reforms and the failed 1991 hardline Communist revolt against his leadership, led by KGB chief Kryuchkov, Kislitsyn's career fell under a cloud. He, like many his age, was suspected of being a Kryuchkov loyalist, which he was not, and a hardcore old-school Communist, which he was.

Kislitsyn, though, was a wily political operator. He survived the demise of the KGB as the various Directorates were split up and new domestic and foreign intelligence services created. He remained my boss in domestic intelligence, both of us now working in the newly formed FSB.

After the rise of Putin, Yeltsin's protégé and surprise choice as successor, Kislitsyn bemoaned that by the year it was getting harder and harder to separate the gangsters from loyal officers in the FSB and rival intelligence agencies. As he faced more and more conflict with various politically appointed superiors he visibly aged as his health deteriorated. Even before he was diagnosed with cancer it was obvious to me that he was in decline.

Most important of all to me though, was that he had helped me deal with the loss of Viktoriya. As a non-smoker, her lung cancer was probably a result of working in the Admiralty shipyard in St. Petersburg, then called Leningrad. I met her there, at a Komsomol dance. Back then, before the risks were understood, she had been exposed to asbestos and other hazardous shipbuilding materials. It was a cruel way to die. Without Kislitsyn to lean on I don't know if I could have coped.

My second vodka did little to quell my rising anger at Kislitsyn's painful end. Viktoriya's death was an accident. Nobody really understood the long-term effects of working with asbestos back then. But the bastards who killed him knew exactly what they were doing. Good, I will need anger to be at my sharpest and to drive me in navigating the dangerous days that lay ahead.

Clarity of thought was brought on by my anger and just the right amount of vodka. First, whoever was interested in following me and in my investigation into Kislitsyn's death would have to show themselves at some point soon to find out exactly what I knew. Second, if they thought it necessary to murder him despite his advancing cancer, they must have come to that conclusion due to a time pressure. Such a time pressure must be connected to one of his investigations, he simply had nothing else. Why else would you want him dead now? Why kill a dying man obsessed with his job as an investigator unless you wanted to prevent him finding out something before his end? Something that you were so desperate to keep quiet you would kill to do so.

Kirilov and I would begin tomorrow by looking into Kislitsyn's active cases at the time of his death. And I knew just the person who could help us with that, a retired archivist the Colonel had been friends with and who we both knew well.

A plan in place and with the help of my vodka I started to relax a little. My attention was brought back into the present by the jeers and cheers of those at the bar. The barman turned the sound up and from the commentary I gathered the referee had just sent off a Dynamo player for diving in an attempt to win a penalty, to the consternation of most of those crowded round the television. Typical, whether in football or life in general the old KGB team was always trying to stick it to it to the Red Army.

Looking up my focus was drawn to the street outside and a new model BMW parked across the way. It didn't belong. In the twilight I could make out the shape and stillness of two people in the front seats. Maybe there had been someone in the shadows back in the park after all.

Fear returned. Over the years I had learned to trust my fear. I finished my vodka, left the lukewarm beer unfinished and without a word slid a couple of notes under the bottle.

Heading for the toilet, out of sight of the entrance, I helped myself to a baseball cap and tracksuit top left unguarded on the uneven coat pegs next to the back door. Quietly I slipped out. Nobody in the bar would have noticed. I prayed the two shadows in the car across the street had not either.

3 CARETAKER

September 22

Bright sunshine fighting through my friend's dirty bedroom curtains woke me. I had a clearer head than usual. The vodka bottle on the side table wasn't empty. I needed my wits about me.

Remembering the shadowy figures in the car outside the Kurant I got out of bed and kept to the wall, peeking through the gap between the window and the drapes at a narrow slice of the world outside. Nothing struck me as out of place, as it hadn't the previous evening on my walk back through the empty side streets. The lack of visible threat brought little comfort. I wondered if my watchers from yesterday had given up and gone home or spent an uncomfortable night observing my apartment from a less obvious vantage point.

Either way I assumed that I was now being watched. It was time for me to play by 'Moscow Rules'. I had first heard that phrase from Kislitsyn who had come across it in a debrief summary report held at the KGB registry. The notes had been made by one of British traitor Kim Philby's handlers in London in the sixties. Philby had said that Moscow was regarded by MI6 as their most difficult operating environment, where it was assumed that any contact with a local was engineered by the KGB or reported to them. MI6 agents operated there with this in mind at all times, always under the assumption of having a tail. This became known among British spies as operating under Moscow Rules. At the height of the Cold War Kislitsyn had been amused by it and had taken to using the phrase himself, as had many of our allies and enemies.

With the rules much in mind I left the apartment by the back stairs to catch a bus to the city center, my normal workday route. My daily journey to the Lubyanka took two busses. The Metro could be quicker but I was in no hurry. I wanted anyone tailing me who had done their homework and knew my routine to make false assumptions about my destination.

Today, as I went to switch busses, I stopped midstride and did an about-face, as if I had forgotten something. I walked with purpose in the direction of the Metro station. Down the stairs and across the platform at a pace suggesting I may perhaps be late for a meeting, but no quicker, I jumped on the train that luckily arrived as I hit the platform. Just beating the closing doors, I pushed my way through the crowd to the middle of the carriage.

The train accelerated. I picked up a copy of Moskovskaya Pravda abandoned by an earlier commuter, making straight for the sports pages. While I maneuvered to apparently get room to read the half open tabloid, I scanned passengers for a tail. I couldn't pick one out. Without my glasses I could still make out the football headlines complaining about a clown of a referee who had cost Dynamo the game.

I found some comfort in the familiarity of my tradecraft, spending the next three hours traveling on trains and buses, all the time aware of my fellow passengers as the rush hour crowds thinned. By eleven thirty I was as confident as I could be that I was no longer being watched.

The thinking time had given me a chance to prioritize the next steps in my investigation. First, find retired KGB archivist Valeri Gerzkov. Second, set up a safe house to work from. I called Kirilov to let him know the plan. He answered after one ring.

"Kirilov."

"Relax, it's me. I need to see an old friend from KGB days this afternoon but will need you tomorrow. How are things there?"

"Quiet. We stayed in for dinner last night. From what I can tell nobody out of the ordinary is hanging around. Tanya's called in sick today and is keeping me company."

I smiled at his hint.

"You two probably need a break. Take Tanya with you and give her cash to pick up two used PC's and a printer from different shops. Make sure to tell her to use the cash, no cards, and you stay out of sight in the car. As soon as you get home disable the Wi-Fi on both and make sure they are clean. I don't want anyone snooping on our work."

"Got it boss. When I'm done, I'll put them back in

Tanya's car and park it away from the apartment."

"Keep an eye out for any goons. I think I had someone watching for me in the neighborhood last night but I think I managed to lose them."

"Will do. You OK?"

"*Khorosho*, I'm fine. I will text you tomorrow morning to arrange a meet. Lay low and keep safe."

"Good luck."

It hit me that Kirilov thought he needed to say that. Christ, we were officers of State Security working in our own country and he was wishing me luck like we were undercover in Syria or somewhere.

The last leg of my merry-go-round to lose any tail had taken me to Paveletsky station, the most ornate of the capital's nine railway terminuses. The station façade dated back to Tsarist days, completed almost twenty years before the October Revolution put an end to such extravagance. The out of place elegance always got me thinking of the past, what it must have been like in the days before the Communists grabbed power.

It was only the screech of brakes and shuddering halt of the train that brought me round from my daydreaming. I jumped off and walked quickly toward the exit heading straight for a taxi, disappearing among the passengers hurrying in all directions at once. Perhaps Kirilov's good luck wishes were working, outside there were a line of cabs and nobody waiting.

"*Zamoskvorechye pozhaluysta*, Zamoskvorechye please."

The taxi driver sped into a gap in the for once fluid traffic in the general direction of Zamoskvorechye. If he was waiting for me to follow up with a street name, he was disappointed. Unperturbed he radioed the dispatcher.

"Two-six. Paveletsky headed Zamoskvorechye. Out".

Seeing I was not one for small talk he turned up the sports channel on the radio. The host was as infuriated with the referee's performance last night as the Pravda sports columnist. I listened to the rant for a couple of minutes before I broke the silence.

"Novokuznetskaya Street".

He nodded an acknowledgment, way more interested in the caller shouting at the radio show guy than me.

We turned on to Novokuznetskaya, a street like many in the area exhibiting slow decay. The residents continued to decline in numbers as one eviction after another made way for office blocks. A couple of the glittering new ones clung to the original building frontages, looming over what soon would be all that remained of the past.

I remembered clearly where Valeri Gerzkov had lived back in the day. Kislitsyn got me to drive them home after their monthly late-night drinking sessions. His flat was right in the middle of the hideous concrete monstrosities that the Soviet had inflicted on the once majestic street in the sixties and seventies.

I called the taxi to a stop a couple of blocks short of my actual destination. He pulled up opposite a still vacant block from where the residents had been evicted years ago. There was no sign of any work on the building they had been kicked out of. These things could take a long time to get started in Moscow, depending on how well connected you were and how many palms you had more than generously greased.

Getting out of the car I walked in the opposite direction to the apartment, reversing only when I saw the taxi driver turn the corner in front of me.

Gerzkov had known Kislitsyn since Khrushchev's days at the top and they had remained firm friends since. On first appearances I had found the archivist boring and unfriendly. But after a few nights out with Kislitsyn and him I learned what a wicked, dry, subversive wit he had. Kislitsyn told me he consciously hid this at work, wanting to appear the humorless, forgettable, state functionary.

Being able to blend into the background was a necessary skill to last as long as he had knowing so many KGB secrets. Gerzkov had survived as long as anybody in the archives, seeing out Stalin and his bloody purges, then surviving the reaction following henchman Lavrentiy Beria's summary arrest and execution.

Gerzkov's preeminent survival instincts meant there was possibly nobody living who knew as much about the secret history of the KGB as him. He had seen as much as anyone, alive or dead, of what had been scrubbed from KGB archive records over the years, or never officially recorded in the first place. Years ago, he told me when much the worse for drink, that once he had been asked for Stalin's personal file from our archives. Apart from the sparse handwritten details on the cover it had been completely empty.

That must have been the only time he didn't come up with the goods. Kislitsyn and I had found him a mine of useful information even after his retirement. We had relied on him for years. The new guard knew little or nothing of Gerzkov and cared even less about him or his generation. That's what him made so valuable to me now, a source of unrivaled knowledge, completely off SVR and FSB radar.

But this usefulness could also be his undoing should the dark forces we were up against need to complete their cover up. People who were willing and able to gun down a high-end property salesman in cold blood in the middle of Moscow, in broad daylight, to keep a secret from someone like me, would have no problem in finishing off the old man. I knew that seeing him was a massive risk, and I felt bad about it, but I was running out of options.

I stopped off at a rundown 24-hour market on the street corner to pick up some pickles and vodka. Entering one of the nearby concrete mausoleums by the rear basement I delivered my gifts to the caretaker who had lived in and looked after the building for decades. I only know her as Elena. I couldn't recall her surname, although I had used her for years. Maybe Kislitsyn never told me. He was so security conscious that he didn't share much about his sources unless he absolutely had to, even with me.

Elena, like so many building caretakers and superintendents in Moscow in those days, was a KGB informer from the start. It went with the territory. Not reporting suspicious behavior and it could be you hauled away in the middle of the night. After years of working with him, when he had grown more confident in my reliability conducting secret domestic KGB investigations, he had gradually introduced me to his networks. Even then, I am sure, not to all of his sources. As for her, he described the dumpy plain woman I was about to meet as one of his favorites, and always considered her a 'most loyal Comrade', from him the highest of praise.

Nothing happened in the neighborhood that Elena didn't know about. She could tell you who was having an affair with who, who was flashing their money around, who had a big mouth and back then who bragged about their illicit pair of Levi's. And all for the price of a peck on the cheek, a smile, a little buttering up and some pickles and vodka.

In later post-Communist years, as the neighborhood set into terminal decline, she could name all the drug runners and lookouts too.

I pushed the half open door at the end of the gloomy corridor.

"*Zdravstvuyte*, hello Elena, how are the damn tenants treating you these days, like a dog as always?"

"Alexander? Alexander, is that you? It's been months, I don't know if I recognize your face, you stay away so long."

She had been in the kitchen. A dark apron covered her dull clothes.

"Ah, pickles and vodka, you are a saint you are, a holy saint like our beloved Major himself, may he rest in peace."

Elena had always referred to Kislitsyn as her 'beloved Major'. He was a Major when she had met him and that is what he would stay.

"What brings you out here, Alexander, what trouble is it now?"

She removed the apron, completing the transition from

caretaker and cleaner to KGB agent.

"No, no, it's nothing like that, no trouble. It's Gerzkov, you know Valeri Gerzkov. I have come to visit and gossip about the old days. I promised him at the funeral I would drop by. Is he still in his old place?"

"*Da tovarishch*, yes comrade. Let me fetch glasses. You know, they will carry him out of there in a box, what with his files and records and books everywhere. No wonder he never married, there's no room for a wife."

I always thought she had had feelings for him. They had remained unrequited.

Elena disappeared behind a curtain and emerged in a heartbeat with two dusty glasses, which she wiped unashamedly with the apron she had just discarded. I had already cracked open the vodka and the pickle jar. She poured two large glasses. It was never too early for her. That is the way it had always been with her debriefs. Motioning to the couch we sat down.

"How is Gerzkov?"

She looked you straight in the eye when answering 'official questions for the protection of the state' from officers like the Major and me. At one time she was a true believer like Kislitsyn and answered routine questions as if the continued security of the Socialist Revolution itself depended solely on her answers. And she knew the drill well.

"He has got old. He hardly comes out these days. His friends have all passed or moved away and he has no family. Although, he did have some visitors the other day."

She couldn't prevent her expression giving away that she knew I would be interested in that. She was an experienced informant.

"What visitors Elena?"

I topped up her vodka in advanced payment for an answer.

She shifted uncomfortably on the ancient sofa, looking every inch her age, her labored movements betraying the years of scrubbing floors and mopping stairwells.

"Police I thought at first, but they were too showy, too smart, too young. I haven't seen Gerzkov to talk to since Saturday, so I don't know for sure, but I would say they were from your new lot – State Security."

She spat out those last words. Elena could not bring herself to acknowledge the demise of the KGB and couldn't bear to say "FSB" or "SVR". She could not understand how they had become separate, rival, security agencies, no matter how often I had explained it.

"Saturday you say, when exactly?"

She straightened at a perceived rebuke from her superior, and hurried to clarify her statement. That was how she had always thought and unlike the times she wouldn't ever change.

"Afternoon... late afternoon, I was just bringing in the last lot of doormats from the fronts which I had left in the sun to dry when they came, and I do that Saturday afternoons to finish the week, so I know."

"How many? Did you recognize them?"

"No Alexander they were mere boys. Two, flashy suits, expensive shoes, new foreign car. Screeched up to the entrance like gangsters in an American movie."

The smile on her face on seeing me was gone. She had turned serious, maybe a little sad.

"They did not even come and ask me questions like the Major and you and any real KGB officer would have done. Damned amateurs. I know things."

I topped our glasses.

"Yes, you do Elena, yes you do. These pups don't know a damned thing, hiding behind their computers all day in their fancy offices. They know nothing about real work in the field. They wouldn't know a good source if they tripped over one in the street."

I had her smiling again. Now she was ready to give her full report, just as formally as she always had done.

"Unidentified male one, late twenties, one point eight meters, cropped dark hair, athletic build. Male two lighter colored mousy-brown hair, a bit shorter, thin, walked with a strange gait like he had been in some sort of accident. Dark colored BMW, looked new. Had two aerials on the roof, one longer than the other."

Elena delivered her report without any pauses, frills or emphasis. An experienced human intelligence source she knew it was not her job to work out what her information meant or tell her handler what was important and what wasn't, just the facts, just what she herself had seen or heard.

I produced a notebook from my coat pocket and wrote down the descriptions carefully. I had been around the block too and I knew that it was important to make your sources feel their information was valuable. You had to make them feel you needed it, even when it was irrelevant gossip. Even diehards like Elena had an ego.

And as always it was in the detail.

"Two aerials you say. No wonder the Major said you were the best in the business. Thank you. So, we know it is them, SVR wouldn't you say?"

Elena gave a small nod before she spoke.

"What would that lot want with Gerzkov these days?"

What indeed. I forced a smile.

"Probably checking he is still alive and that a squatter isn't claiming his pension. You know what, I'll ask him directly what business he has hanging round with men in fancy suits, driving new German cars."

I left despite Elena's entreaties for me to stay and finish the bottle, like we would have done in the old days. I know she liked a drink but I think she craved the company more. I used the tried and tested 'matters of state security' excuse to make good my escape. For once though, I wasn't lying.

Elena had set alarm bells ringing in my head. Why after all these years had two SVR goons decided now was a good time to come and see an almost forgotten former KGB archivist who just happened to be one of Kislitsyn's lifelong best friends?

4 ARCHIVIST

I was not surprised to find most of the lights were out in the dingy stairwell of Gerzkov's building. He lived on the third floor and there was no elevator, which was no help for my knees. Moving along the hallway I could sense that I was being watched. Only this time it was the twitching curtains of neighbors. I guess nowadays there weren't as many visitors as there used to be. I was conscious that it might be paranoia that led me to wonder if one of the nosy neighbors had been asked to keep an eye out for visitors to Gerzkov's apartment. Then again, with what I had seen and heard these last few days, it was more than possible. The closer I got to his apartment the more I could feel my stomach knotting.

Stopping at the second to last door I took a deep breath and tried to calm myself before I knocked. There was no doorbell. After a few moments I knocked again, louder, then bent down and pushed the letterbox open.

"Gerzkov, its Danilov, Alexander Danilov. Valeri my

friend it's me, Alexander."

Hearing the mumbled reply and shuffling feet inside I closed my eyes and let out a long breath, my very worst fears allayed at least.

"Alright, alright, I'm coming. What's with the shouting, this is a quiet neighborhood. You know, I am not so quick on my feet these days."

The door opened part way. Gerzkov looked over his half-moon reading glasses to check I was who I said I was. He appeared to have stopped aging. He looked old, but the same old as twenty years ago.

"Alexander. When you said you would call after the funeral, I thought it would be in a few days, or weeks. You leave it until now? I could be in the grave already."

The words may have been harsh but the tone was friendly. I could tell he was pleased to see me.

"I've been busy, you know how it is."

"I know how it is. Busy is it? Busy, blah, blah, blah. Busy was when we had the CIA at our throats and lunatics in the White House threatening Cuba, that my friend, that was busy."

He rarely missed a chance to reminisce about the glory days at the height of the Cold War. Stepping in, he had already turned and was walking back to the living room, still muttering to himself. He had never been one for handshakes or even worse in his estimation, a hug or a kiss on the cheeks.

He had lived alone for years now. Stormy, the ironically

named lazy black tomcat that had always been around his feet had died a few years ago, his last real excuse for talking to himself gone.

I thought I picked out 'you can close it' among the grumbling. Newly security conscious I bolted the door and put the chain on.

Catching him up he pointed at an old sofa for me to sit as he headed to the kitchen. I heard him put the kettle on for tea. There were papers and files everywhere. Piled high on the sideboard, the dining table and the floor. I moved the open file on the small couch aside, careful to keep it open on the same page. Odd words and sentences had been highlighted in a garish yellow. Comments had been hand written in the margin in a faultless beautiful script. There was a mug shot of a scarred man with a near shaven head. He caught me inspecting the file.

"Bereshenko, Alexi, small time drug dealer, local. You know him?"

"Not really, but I've heard of him. He died last year in a gang thing."

"That's what they say."

He didn't seem at all convinced, but didn't elaborate.

"Now Alexander, which is it, social call, chat about old hoods or something else?"

"To be honest I think it's a little of all three. Why don't you just get on with making my tea like a proper host would and we can get down to business when you have."

He permitted himself a smile at my pretense of

indignation and made for the kitchen without another word, returning with two steaming hot glasses of tea.

I was ready with my questions. He would know as little as I needed him to know and no more. The old man's safety was important to me. There were few from the service that I had grown to respect more.

"I am just looking to close out Kislitsyn's last few cases. I thought you could help me with one or two things, if anyone can."

"*Konechno*, sure, if I can. What do you need to know?"

"We have received a letter, but it's not clear what case it relates to. Do you know if he was working on anything special towards the end? You met him regularly then, did he mention anything in particular?"

"Nothing major that I recall. He was distracted in those last months. He seemed more reticent than usual. What kind of case are you thinking of? Criminal? Internal? Juicy?"

"I wish I was sure. You know how he was, a devil for not filing reports properly or keeping records. When I accessed the main computer index with his ID I got hardly anything about his recent investigations, with some folders completely empty. He had either not saved anything or deleted it. For such a tidy mind his record keeping was a complete mess."

He couldn't keep his laughter in. He had made the same complaints about me for years.

"The pair of you made our jobs in records a nightmare. But let's not speak ill of the dead. I did jot down one or two things he asked me for late on. You work on your tea and I'll dig out my notes."

He began sifting through the piles of papers on the dining table. How he knew where to start I will never know.

Unlike Kislitsyn, Gerzkov would never get out of the habit of recording everything in one way or another. It was his business. For him intelligence didn't exist until it was written down, graded, classified, indexed and filed.

Finished, I collected up the glasses and headed to the kitchen to boil more water for another. Next to the samovar was a bottle of Cuban rum. He seemed to think it was an essential ingredient ever since Kislitsyn brought one back as a present from some mission there. I was never sure if the rum was to disguise the taste of the terrible tea he was addicted to or the tea was to take the edge off the rum.

By the time I returned he had put his reading glasses on and was engrossed with a notepad with bright yellow pages. He had move to the sofa and patted the seat next to him for me to sit down.

"Nothing too interesting I'm afraid Alexander. More internal type matters than big interesting cases. He asked me who would have held on to KGB property records after the SVR, FSB, split. I told him which Departments would have kept what, but when I asked if he wanted me to reach out and find out more, he told me it was not important and not to bother. I have to admit he was a bit abrupt, although at the time I put that down to him being in so much pain. It seemed to come over him in waves. By then he should have been at home, saving what strength he had left. He didn't ask me about the property records again, so I let it drop."

"But nothing specific, no direct questions, no case names or suspect individuals?"

"No, nothing like that. We spent the rest of the time just reminiscing about old times. Mainly gossip, like who had got on since the old days and who hadn't. You know the kind of thing, who had a big house now or a new dacha. I found it a bit of an odd conversation between us, because as you know he wasn't exactly one for that kind of nonsense and had never cared a jot about where people lived or how fancy their house was."

This was not what I wanted to hear. I could feel one of my main hopes for a break in the case fading fast. I tried not to let my disappointment show by sharing some of the latest juicy FSB gossip with him. He got a gig kick out of the false rumors about Kirilov's sexuality.

We had finished our tea, which seemed to signal the end of our meeting. He stood up and led me towards the door.

"Now it's time for you to go and be busy again."

"Thank you, my friend. Back to see if I can make any sense of Kislitsyn's computer files, which you know won't be easy!"

"I know, I know, and his scribbling in those notebooks he had taken up with."

I stopped dead and turned to face the old man the door chain still in hand.

"What notebooks? Kislitsyn was obsessive about

security. He never kept a personal note in his life."

"No, you are quite right, for years he never did. But near the end he confided to me that he feared his memory was failing him and he began to write things down. He kept a notebook and pen with him whenever he called in those last months. He jotted things down even as we gossiped about the old days."

"I just can't picture him with a notebook and pencil like a provincial flatfoot."

"Yes, he was not himself at all at the end, he really wasn't. Like he had something big on his mind but he just couldn't let it out. Anyway, I am sorry I could not be more help."

"It was a long shot. I am sure there was nothing too important with that letter we got. I will close out his last cases as best I can. Now I have to go. It was really good to see you."

"Don't leave it so long next time."

"I won't, I promise. And do me a favor, check in with Elena from time to time, she is getting on and needs keeping an eye on. *Do svidaniya.*"

"*Do svidaniya.*"

I descended the stairs as quickly as my knees would let me, not letting go of the handrail. Christ, all of a sudden, I am beginning to feel more like one of the old man's generation than Kirilov's.

Gerzkov may have apologized for not being able to help but he had been far more useful than he realized.

Letting him know that though would put him danger. He was best not knowing much at all.

There was no way that Kislitsyn had suddenly become a gossip and he definitely didn't give a damn about anybody's fancy dacha. I didn't buy the failing memory bit either. He may well have been in a lot of pain at the end, but whenever I spoke to him, he was clearly as sharp as a tack.

No, he must have had a good reason to be sniffing around who from the old guard had come into property and how. He was on to something. I could smell it. And what's with those notebooks?

I had never seen Kislitsyn with the little notebooks Gerzkov described, not in the office, not in the car, not anywhere. I had cleared out his desk personally, I simply couldn't face anyone else rummaging through his things. No, he wasn't writing those notes for himself, his memory was as good as ever, whatever act he put on for Gerzkov. So, if he wasn't taking notes as a reminder for himself, what was he taking them for? I simply had to find them. He must have kept them at home.

Now there was the problem. He had never actually owned his own place. He had always lived in the apartment that came with the job. To be fair KGB Colonels mostly got nice apartments. But now, no doubt, his old place was someone else's. Whoever was in his apartment was bound to have cleared his things out.

And there is only one person who would have received his belongings, his daughter Irina. Damned kid hated me and anyone else from the office almost as much as she hated him. Surely, she wouldn't have just dumped his things though, not even her. There was only one way to find out, although the prospect of another of Irina's lectures was not something I was looking forward to.

By deciding to make his own records of cases and keep them at home he was breaking every rule in his own book. That had to be for a damn good reason. Maybe he didn't want anyone in the office seeing the notebooks. That was it. He didn't trust any of them with the investigations he was working on.

He must have suspected someone in the office was involved, he must have done. Fuck, he must have suspected me too. Jesus, whatever he had found that had gotten him killed was something to do with one of us.

I needed to let Kirilov know that the danger was probably from someone in the Russian Intelligence Services that we knew. We couldn't trust anyone. I had to get back, now.

After an uneventful but painfully long journey on a near empty bus back to the City center I headed for a student hangout I knew from drug investigations. I got a beer and chose a corner table facing the entrance, easing myself down to the way too low sofa. The payphone I was looking for was on the back wall, surrounded with taxi numbers and colorful escort invitations. No doubt mob run the lot of them. Halfway through my beer I made the call.

"*Privet*".

"It's me. Our friend from the archives gave me a lead. How did things go with you?"

"All sorted, wireless disabled, hard-drives scrubbed and ready to go. In the back of Tanya's car. It's parked two blocks away around the back of her friends work, nice spot, secluded."

"Perfect. Take her car and meet me tomorrow morning at ten outside that dive bar the boys go to after work, you know the one, with the pretty Estonian barmaid?"

"I know it."

"Tomorrow at ten then, and stay outside. We have a few busy days ahead of us. Tell Tanya you will be out of town for the week."

"Okay boss."

"And Kirilov, listen to me carefully. From what I found out today the men we are after could be in the FSB or SVR or both, they could even be in our office. Trust nobody, hear me, nobody."

I put the phone down before Kirilov had chance to ask any difficult questions. I didn't want to say too much on an open line.

With nothing to do until the meeting tomorrow I had time to relax and enjoy a quiet beer for once. A boatload of noisy students put paid to that. Time to scoot.

Hailing the first taxi that came into view, I paid no mind that it was going in the opposite direction to the station. To speed up the driver and make it difficult for a tail I made out I was late for a train and promised a generous tip. Moscow Rules. The taxi shot into a U-turn and accelerated well past the speed limit. From the back seat I didn't pick out any other reckless driving.

Two draining hours later, with evasive bus and train

journeys behind me, I was back at my apartment building. I had decided this would be my last night there. Time to shake the tree and send them a message.

5 GOING DARK

September 23

Today the sunrise had no chance to wake me. I'd hardly slept. There was so much to do. I had to force myself to take a breath, calm down and just focus on one task at a time.

First a cup of my friend's Italian coffee, sent over from Germany by his son, which we had shared on occasion. The coffeepot spluttered on the hob, not yet done, so I carefully moved the blind a half inch from the window and took a peek out. A man by the phone box across the street showing little interest in making a call and far more focus on the apartment windows above me.

The pot reached a crescendo so I grabbed it off the heat and poured a mug. Watching the man for a while and sipping my coffee I waited to see if he bothered to feign a call or not. He didn't.

They wanted me to spot them. They were trying to put the pressure on, hoping for me to come in and tell them exactly how much I knew and who else I had been speaking to. Well, two can play at that game.

Topping up and taking my mug with me I dressed in the same shirt and trousers I had worn last night. My knees bothered me as I sat on the low bed to put my shoes and socks on. The miles I was walking on counter surveillance may be doing my weight good but it was playing havoc with my joints. I needed to get a move on. Back in the kitchen I poured some cold water in my mug and slugged it back.

I took the back stairs up to my floor not wanting to risk the elevator. I didn't pass anyone in the stairwell or corridor. Turning the key slowly and carefully I eased my door open and listened. Nothing. Despite all my curtains and blinds being closed I daren't put a light on.

I worked in the dimness of my bedroom, illuminated only from the gap between the drooping curtains and the rail. From the bottom of my small wardrobe I removed the sports bag and checked the side pocket for my passport, false identification papers and credit cards. Some of the credit cards were in my name, others were in undercover names I had got for missions long past, but never used. They were clean. I picked out the ones I knew I had used before and tossed them on the bed.

There was no need to check the rest of the sports bag. Standard contents included two shirts, one spare tie, one pair of trousers, a sweater, two pairs army grade wool socks, underwear, razor, toothbrush and shower gel. The clothes smelt a bit musty. I couldn't remember the last time I worked on a case urgent enough for me to have to grab my ready bag.

I took my battle-scarred Czech made Carl Zeiss 35mm camera off the wardrobe shelf and grabbed the spare films beside it. It had been everywhere with me and had the dints and scratches to prove it. With the lens fitted it was heavier than I remembered, having got used to the new digital ones from the office. It was bigger too, taking up half the remaining space in the bag.

In the gloom I levered up the wooden boards at the bottom of the wardrobe using an old door handle I kept on one of the shelves expressly for this. Reaching into the darkness I removed the false bottom and retrieved the money. Five clear plastic moneybags with rolled up wads of notes, one thousand US dollars in each. Yankee dollars remained the standard of those on the run, taken everywhere, whatever the crisis. The only thing I really knew for certain about this damned investigation was how much I had to pay for it.

I took all five bags, my entire life savings, and put them deep into my inside coat pockets. Reaching further back in the dark space beyond the gap in the boards I felt the oily cloth that I kept round my unregistered Makarov pistol. Taking it out I cocked it and checked the mechanism, not the least surprised all was in working order. Regular cleaning and maintenance had been drummed into me by my father.

He said he had won the gun in a card game but I long suspected he had confiscated it when he was on border guard duty and kept it for himself, for a rainy day. Metaphorically for me right now it was pouring. Having his trusted firearm in my hand right now was a comfort, not just for what it could do, but because it had been his. Mother hated having it around the house, but she had kept it for me until she thought I was old enough to be trusted.

I was in the KGB myself by then.

That was everything. Now it was time to escape the attentions of my watchers and go dark until this was over. Grabbing my bag and coat I headed to the kitchen and turned the three gas burners on my stove full on. Forcing a rolled-up newspaper into my electric toaster I kept it jammed and heating. I avoided looking at the picture of Viktoriya and me above the table. Now there was no time for a last look around home before I slammed the door behind me. That would have broken me.

A few yards down the hallway I smashed the fire alarm in the corridor and shouted 'Fire' at the top of my voice. Almost immediately doors started to open and residents emerged into the corridor.

"Out! Out! Quickly, Out!"

Others joined in raising the alarm. I went on banging doors and making as much fuss as I could all the way to the back stairs. By the time I got to the bottom of the last flight I heard the explosion and the glass from apartment windows smashing to the ground outside.

I took the fire warden's vest from my coat pocket and put it on. As people began to stream out of my block, I spotted my chance. An old lady was struggling to keep pace with the flow of people rushing by. As I pushed my way through, she took my arm gratefully and I led her to the rear yard of the building. Signs throughout directed residents to congregate there in emergencies.

Forcing the old lady on a neighbor no more than a few years her junior I headed back into a block to help someone else, by all appearances a conscientious fire warden. This time I entered the building on the opposite side of the courtyard from my own.

I made my way down toward the basement shouting for anyone left behind. Getting no reply, I discarded the fluorescent vest and took the baseball cap out of my pocket that I stole from the bar, pulling it as far down as it would go. Back up the stairs to the ground floor I left through the front entrance. Slowing my pace, I disappeared among the growing crowd of residents and onlookers as the first fire engines noisily announced their arrival.

I made an effort to calm my breathing and not rush. One street over, a policeman had blocked the road to through traffic, only letting emergency vehicles pass. As I got closer, I could hear an argument. The baby-faced cop had stopped a taxi collecting a ride from a nearby apartment building. The anti-surveillance gods were on my side today.

My offer of an alternative fare quickly accepted I gave the driver the name of a Metro station in the direction the traffic was moving best. A final burst of expletives to the law as he floored the accelerator, speeding us away from the chaos I had caused.

I gave the still simmering driver a good tip, but got no confirmation his mood had remotely improved. Knowing I had time on my hands I ignored the stairs to the Metro and headed across the street to the nearest bus stop, not caring where I was headed. Two minutes later a bus drew up. As soon as the doors opened everyone rushed to get on at the same time. It was a matter strength, timing and luck as to who boarded first and got a seat. I kept out of it. Back when I was in London, I had been amazed that people mostly stood in line for buses and took their turn to get on. That was years ago now, but even back then there was no chance of such order in Moscow.

I left it late and just as the driver moved for the handle to close the door, I sprang forward blocking the door with one hand and squeezed on. The driver glared at me. I ignored him and pushed my way through the crowd toward the back seat, surveying the passengers for a familiar face or anyone looking out of place. I prayed my stunt at the apartment building and the fortuitous appearance of the taxi had been enough to throw my tail. I had an hour to kill before I met Kirilov so time for two or three random bus changes and some more serious focus on the faces of my fellow passengers. You never know, it may have worked.

Forty-five minutes later I mentally declared myself black. The second switch had been quick, there was hardly anyone on the third bus and nobody else got off at my stop. I was as sure as I could be. I looked at my watch, there was time. At a steady pace I cut across the corner of Tagansky Park, forcing myself again to slow down and not be early to meet Kirilov.

Approaching the meeting point from the east corner I could see the car Kirilov had described parked in a side street. As I got close, I was happy to see he must have been paying attention to his mirrors, the door springing open before me.

"*Dobroye utro*, good morning boss."

"*Dobroye utro*."

"All quiet?"

"Yes, and with you?"

"Nothing."

"Good. Let's get to work. Danilovsky District. Take the Third Ring Road. There is one of those American hotel chains there. I have used it before. We have direct access to the ring road and it's only a short walk to the Metro at Avtozavodskaya."

"Our new home?"

"For the next few days anyway."

The hotel was perfect. The website showed it was popular with tourists and businessmen on a budget, included free high-speed internet, free parking and only one hundred and fifty rooms or so in total. Lower profile but busy. Who would notice us here among the not so successful businessmen hawking their dubious wares around the capital? Six miles from the Kremlin, it may as well have been six hundred. As long as we move every few days and keep our heads down it could be a while before they found us. That said a ready cover story wouldn't do us any harm.

While Kirilov hid Tanya's car amongst the shiny rentals in the rear car park I checked us in. The hassled receptionist paid me little attention as the Turkish businessman she was checking in shouted something about a special rate in poor Russian, as if the extra volume would help her understand. Positioning myself alongside at the counter I passed her a knowing look and rolled my eyes. She smiled and without a word took and swiped my credit card, then passed me a key, all without taking her eyes off the irate Turk for any more than a second.

The fob was boldly engraved '115', suggesting they had actually read my email request for a ground floor room. Nice to have the option of an easy window exit if needed.

The large sports bag Kirilov had handed me was heavy. Not surprising as it contained a computer and flat screen monitor packed in among what I presumed were old clothes from Tanya's place. That was smart of him. He was learning fast. With only the stuffed sports bags as luggage it wouldn't look like we were about to set up a functioning investigations office in a bedroom. Moreover, this was the kind of place where a 'do not disturb' sign would be a welcome sight to the overworked cleaners. We should be able to work in peace for a day or two at least.

Leaving him assembling the computers, I headed out the hotel through the back door, leading to the car park. It was helpfully unmanned and accessed by keycard. My run of luck continued. Before I was halfway through my cigarette, I found a public phone that hadn't been vandalized. Forgetting my glasses, I had some difficulty dialing the number from my pocket address book, squinting at the jumbled digits. I made my best guess and was again fortunate.

"*Privet*, Hello."

"Hello old friend, how are you coping with all that sunshine."

On the other end of the line Sergei stifled a laugh.

"Fine, it's good for my old bones you scoundrel. What's up?"

Sergei was a suspicious old spy. He never used names on open lines when he didn't have to. And he knew I was after a favor.

"You know me too well. I need to throw someone off my scent."

"Trouble?"

"Don't worry, it's no worse than usual. I just need to be left alone for a few days if you know what I mean."

The reply was instant.

"What do you need?"

"A little smoke. Take one of my cards, go to an internet café that takes cash and book me a train from Moscow. I think I need some of that Crimean sunshine too."

"Economy I think, you don't deserve any better."

"Perfect. You know I'm cheap! Oh, and be my guest for a few days. Take the family out for dinner, spend a little, my treat."

"Sure, my pleasure."

Sergei knew I wasn't just being kind, but hoped a few meals may make someone believe, at least for a while, that I had actually taken the train.

"This summer I will come for real. I promise."

I had sworn I would at least half a dozen times, but never been.

"You are always welcome, always, my friend."

"I know, I know, just one more thing."

"What?"

"*Byt' ostorozhen*, be careful."

Sergei hung up without another word. In the seconds before he did, I could feel his concern.

6 IRINA

The door to the hotel room opened before I had time to insert the keycard. With mock pride Kirilov handed me a test page off the printer. The two computers and monitors were set up in front of the flat screen TV.

 "Password looks like Moscow#1, so we can remember it, keeping a capital 'M', but with zero twice replacing the letter 'O'. One thumb drive in each so we don't have to save anything at all to the hard drives. In an emergency we can grab them and run."

"No need to erase anything from the memory?"

"There will be stuff that can be recovered from the memory given time but it will slow them down. I have installed a virus that will corrupt the entire memory if you don't input the correct password when prompted. It will pop up every thirty minutes or so when the computer is in use. The password is the same one I just gave you. No need to make it too easy for anyone to see what we have been up to."

"Pull the thumb drives while I sort out where we're going."

Inside the wardrobe was a small digital safe. I placed four rolls of cash and the camera without lens in and locked it. I squeezed the telescopic lens in the bedside table next to a suspiciously new looking bible.

"We need to find Kislitsyn's daughter at Moscow State University. Let's start with the main campus. Head west on the Third Ring Road. It's only twenty minutes."

"Moscow State, I know it. What do we need with his kid?"

"I'm afraid she may be the only person that can help us, though she will not want to. She hated her father for doing this job and despises us. And the less she knows the better, not only for her own safety, but she's, shall we say, political."

The drive took forty-five minutes rather than twenty, a stalled bus on the ring road seeing to that. I told Kirilov to follow signs for the University Registrar's office so we could find out Irina's address. I remembered from talking to Kislitsyn that she lived on campus but I had no idea where.

"Pull up here. Its best if you ask the Registrar. Questions from a big shot like me could raise a few eyebrows. Tell them it's in relation to a student protest application. No doubt Irina will be involved with those. Mention the Navalny corruption protests, that should throw them off. They have probably had dozens of inquiries from us lately. Remind them Irina is doing a degree in Media Studies."

"Got it, Media Studies."

Kirilov rolled his eyes. I don't think he was impressed with the choice of course.

He jumped out and headed for the Registrar's office. I had time for a quick look around at the campus. Surrounded by parkland the university was near the Sparrow Hills which overlooked the new Luzhniki Stadium and the Kremlin beyond. Some signs and flags survived from 'Russia 2018', the football World Cup. Generally, the tournament had been well received abroad. For once a positive moment in the international limelight, before GRU election interference in the US had returned things to normal.

Not long after I returned to the car Kirilov showed up with a smug look on his face and handed me a sticky note. 'Irina Kislitsyn' and an address written in a neat hand, beside what seemed from the capitalization something important to the Registrar's assistant at least: 'THIRD YEAR - Media Studies'. Irina in the third year already. Jesus, time flies.

"The assistant was very friendly. I think she had a thing for me. Anyway, in the small talk I got out of her that no other 'officials' had been nosing around asking questions about Irina. That information cost me my phone number, but seeing as my cellphone is presently lost in an old Audi or in some thief's pocket somewhere in Moscow, who cares."

The address on the note was only a few minutes away and as it was another beautiful day we walked. The campus accommodation blocks were clearly signed and when we got to the right one the door had been propped open. Perhaps the ground floor students were hoping to catch a cool breeze.

He slowed to my pace after the first flight, not wanting to show me up too much, just enough to make a point. On the next landing I checked the note again and found 'A3-15', a few doors down. I rapped on the door with my best policeman's knock, right next to a Pussy Riot poster. The words 'Fuck Putin' had been scrawled across the top in red marker pen, just in case you didn't get the message. There was no mistaking that this was Irina's room.

An unshaven hollow-eyed youth opened the door. Kirilov jumped in first.

"Is Irina Kislitsyn here? This is her room, right?"

He looked us both up and down before he replied. My first impression, skinny but not callow.

"Yes, it's her room but she's out. At a seminar."

"And you are?"

"Stefan, her boyfriend. What's this about, is she in trouble?"

It sounded like he was used to that. I spoke before he could continue.

"Trouble, no, no, what makes you think that Stefan? No, I am an old friend of her father's. I just wanted a quick word with her. I promised him I would check in every now and again and make sure she was ok. Do you know when she will be back?"

"About an hour I think, why don't you come back in…"

I didn't wait for him to finish, taking a bold step forward I left him little choice but to open the door the rest of the way and retreat inside.

"We will wait, thanks. Cigarette?"

Kirilov moved jeans, t-shirts and underwear from one armchair for me and sat himself down on the end of the bed, giving a cigarette to Stefan.

Kirilov's turn.

"Have you known her long?"

An old razor and shaving foam alongside a collection of female grooming products on the small hand basin by the dresser suggested long enough.

"Since the first year."

"That's good, I am glad she has a steady young man with her. Especially with losing her father, my commanding officer and comrade of many years, like she did."

He colored, maybe embarrassed by what I had said, stubbing out his barely started cigarette.

"She hated him! She never even mentions him."

This time I produced the cigarettes, lighting one for Stefan in an effort to calm him down.

"Stefan, I have known Irina since the day she was born. She was always a strong-willed character, and as she got older, she was never comfortable with her father's work with the services. Did you ever meet him?"

"Once or twice near the end. He came here to see her but

she wouldn't even talk to him. She made me send him away. It was awful. I couldn't talk her round."

I was beginning to warm to the young man. He had least attempted to get Irina to build some bridges with her father when she knew he was dying.

"Your parents, they are well?"

"I don't know them. I was adopted. When I was called up for my national service, I cut all contact with my foster parents. They weren't kind to me."

"I'm sorry to hear that Stefan."

"Don't be. They were cold and distant and I had no real feelings for them. Until my national service in the army and then Irina, I never really had family."

"She likes lost causes."

He smiled at my joke. The tension eased.

Stefan could be useful. Without his encouragement I doubted she would even speak to us. Picking up on his mention of national service I told him about my early days in the Red Army and my first meeting with Irina's father, which hadn't gone well. Kirilov was smart enough to follow my lead and keep the conversation going in that direction.

"Where did you serve?"

"An infantry brigade on the Ukraine border, not far from Donbass. I am still in touch with my army buddies. We are close, and I can see them being lifelong friends, maybe like you and the Colonel."

I liked it that Stefan referred to Irina's father by rank.

The friendly conversation didn't last. The unlocked door swung open and Irina bounded into the room. She stared open mouthed at us.

"What the fuck do you want?"

"*Zdravstvuyte*, Hello, Irina. I need your help."

I had planned to hide the purpose of our visit behind the guise of a welfare check on my best friend's only daughter. Seeing the look on Irina's face I knew that was pointless.

Irina just stood there.

"Just one quick question, then we'll go. Before your father died, he started keeping his own notes on his cases, I believe in little black notebooks. I need to find them, now. Do you know where they are?"

"You think I would help you and your corrupt Putin puppet friend here, even if I knew what the hell you were talking about? You are even more stupid than I remember."

I had to tell her more, much as I didn't want to.

"It may sound melodramatic but I am trying to follow a message your father left me from beyond the grave, to finish something he thought was really important. He was a good man Irina, and this is to do with corrupt officials of the worst kind, real Putin puppets to a man. He left a trail for me to pick up for a reason. He must have known he was in some sort of danger and I am not going to let his memory down."

Stefan went to speak, but cut she him off.

"Well, even if I wanted to help you I couldn't. I threw out all the things he left for me. I didn't even look at them. Now if you don't have a warrant, I demand that you leave. *Teper*, Now!"

Kirilov looked angry but I jumped in before he could make it worse.

"Ok we're leaving. But tell me this, where and when did you throw your father's things away, was it here at the University?"

This time Stefan cut in.

"I put them out for the cleaners to take. There are some large bins at the end of each corridor."

"When was this, do you remember?"

"His stuff was delivered by his attorney, well an assistant of his anyway, maybe a week or two after he passed away."

Irina glared at Stefan. "You have your answer, now go, and don't come back."

She opened the door for us to leave. We obeyed knowing she would tell us nothing. I turned back.

"Take care of yourself Irina."

She slammed the door.

As we walked away down the corridor in silence, we could hear Irina and Stefan's raised voices but could not make out what they were yelling at each other. Kirilov shrugged as we hit the stairs.

Pausing at the bottom of the stairwell to light another cigarette and collect my thoughts I heard footsteps skipping down the concrete steps behind us. Stefan was out of breath when he caught up.

"I didn't want to say but I didn't throw her father's stuff out, I couldn't. One day she will want it, I'm sure of that."

"*Gde*? where?"

"There are two boxes in my car, behind the block. That's all. I can show you."

He led us around the corner to a walkway between the drab buildings leading to the parking lot. In the far corner was a dark green Soviet-era Lada. Taking the keys, he fiddled with the lock and eventually the trunk sprung open with a groan. Peering inside I was relieved to see two neat looking cardboard boxes, labeled "Kislitsyn", the printed labels clearly the work of the attorney's office rather than the Colonel.

"Help yourself."

My heart was pounding as I removed the lid. In the first there was nothing but personal papers and legal papers, neatly saved in clear plastic folders. Kirilov had picked the second box up and balanced it on the edge of the trunk, leaving me to open it, knowing how eager I was. Immediately I could see it was more promising. An untidy collection the attorney's office clearly had less interest in and didn't know what to make of.

I shifted the personal photos off the top and there they

were. Three small black notebooks, just as Gerzkov had described. I scooped them up and slipped all three carefully in my inside jacket pocket without even opening the cover.

"Thank you, Stefan. This is just what we were looking for. I can't tell you what this is all about or how important it is but I can tell you it's about doing the right thing for the Colonel. Just like you would for your army buddies. Please keep the rest of this stuff for Irina. As you said, she will want it one day."

He smiled thinly and nodded.

"Stefan you are good for her. Do me a favor and just keep an eye on her for me".

I ripped a page from the back of my old address book and wrote down the burner phone number.

"Call me if you need anything, but don't give this number to anyone else, not even Irina."

As a fellow Red Army veteran, even though a very young one, I thought a fair warning wouldn't rattle him.

"And if anyone else comes sniffing around asking about Irina's father, anyone at all, say nothing and give me a call right away."

Shaking hands, he headed back to face the music and we returned to the main campus, co-conspirators in a secret pact to try and keep Irina safe. I walked as quickly as I could. I couldn't wait to get back to the hotel and finally see what was in those damned notebooks. Whatever it was, it had likely got my best friend killed.

7 NOTEBOOKS

The drive back to our hotel took eighteen minutes. Kirilov drove and was as keen to read the notebooks as I was. When we got there, I exerted my authority and sent him for coffee so I could get a head start.

I glanced through Kislitsyn's scribbled notes in the three small journals. It didn't take long. The notebooks were the size of my hand, black covered, with no labels, only a brand name embossed in the middle of the back cover, which I couldn't make, out even with my glasses on. They were of European or American quality, and I counted exactly thirty pages. Most were blank. The printed lines on the pages were narrow, so anyone with eyes as bad as mine would write on every other line, just as Kislitsyn had.

Through the pages his handwriting betrayed his worsening illness. The sight of the scrawl on what I presume was the last book pained me. Starting back on the first, I took my time and began to read. He had a headline, and a case name, followed by an FSB format case number on the next line. The jotted notes followed in date order, then a number of blank pages before the next case notes began. I inferred his investigations were incomplete, with room to document updates for each. So, he was maybe working on more than one case at the same time, possibly they were interlinked.

Kirilov's return with coffee cut short my theorizing.

"I will take the last notebook; you take these two. Don't rush, I want a detailed reading of each case. Take notes, highlight anything that strikes you as familiar, unusual or needs to be followed up on."

"Sure thing, you're the boss. We should make a separate folder on the thumb drive for each case. Tonight, I will copy my folders on to yours and yours onto mine."

"Agreed. And a third thumb drive backup for the prosecutor."

He settled at the desk to read the notebooks and type his comments up. Betraying age I settled on the bed and grabbed a pen and paper to put down my thoughts by hand as I worked. He wouldn't like it but he could type mine up for me later.

For over an hour we worked without a word. Kirilov swapped notebooks. He was working more quickly than me. I had to ask.

"Anything?"

"Nothing jumps out. Small-time stuff, some I know about already. Most of it was dealt with the old way rather than prosecuted. The good news is that it won't take me long to check it all out. You got anything?"

"Nothing much, just routine cases like yours, two bribery and one theft of state property. Do you remember that one last summer, the idiot sergeant selling drugs taken from the evidence room back to dealers?"

"I remember it. The first dealer we picked up couldn't wait to sell him out for a reduced sentence."

"Keep working. I am sure we will know what we are looking for when we see it."

Fifteen minutes later I found it.

In the second half of my notebook after a number of blank pages Kislitsyn had changed his note taking style. The notes were short, not in Cyrillic characters, just single words and numbers. There were three consecutive pages with a few words and some numbers on each.

MANOR RUBLEVKA
7,800 sq
POA
CY0000000000000535297652453

Rubin Estate
$1,066,293
LT0000000000000537854432435

COTTAGE VILLAGE LETOVO
$2,000,000
LT0000000000000535297652453

"Kirilov, what do you make of this?"

He grabbed my notebook, tiring of what he had been reading in his. I stood up and walked to the window to get a cigarette and stretch my legs. I was only just lighting it when he replied.

"I guess property for sale and values, maybe along with some sort of reference number?"

"And in English not Russian like the rest of the notes."

"This is something."

"Agreed. Do me a favor. Take my notes from the bed, set up the computer folders and type them up for me. I have to go out and make a call. And start with the three English pages, they look the most promising."

"Will do. Bring some food back, I'm starving."

"I'll get donuts and you can pretend to be a real cop."

He made a salute and was muttering something in a bad American accent but the creaking hotel door behind me drowned him out. Slow down, think. This time I would leave by the front entrance and use a different public phone than last time. Not much, but we had to be as security conscious as we could.

Then I saw them.

There were two. Plain clothes men talking to the receptionist. They were leaning over the counter, engrossed in what was on the screen. I took a chance that they hadn't seen me, managed to keep control, turned around and maintained a casual stride back to the elevator bank. Turning the corner, I ran down the corridor as fast as I could and burst through our door.

"We're leaving, now. Grab the thumb drives and what you

can in thirty seconds, then we're gone."

Kirilov sprang up from his chair and got to work on the computers while I grabbed the notebooks and my hand written notes and stuffed the lot in my coat pockets. I took the camera, lens and money from their hiding places and threw them in a sports bag, folding the other empty one inside, yanking the zipper closed.

"*Poydem*, let's go."

We had been quick. We might just get away with it. I handed him the sports bag and put my baseball cap on. He pulled his hood up as we walked quickly down the corridor. Both of us turned away from the security camera as we headed out the back exit.

Kirilov had the knack and got Tanya's old car started first time. As we drove by the front of the hotel, I stole a glance. A new top of the range black BMW saloon was parked across the entrance. Reception was now empty apart from the staff behind the counter. We had made it out just in time.

I couldn't be a hundred percent sure they were looking for us, but it was too much of a coincidence. People like me didn't believe in coincidences. People like me didn't believe in much. But more important than belief, my experience demanded that I think, if they could have been looking for us, then act like they were looking for us. That's how you stay alive.

"Where now?"

For the first time his voice had an edge of doubt, a suggestion of fear.

"Head for the city. Let's go shopping. These SVR grunts

are predictable. If they were trawling the hotels looking for us, they would probably have started in the city center at the better hotels and worked their way out. We will head in the opposite direction. Let's ditch the car and take the Metro, I am not sure if the hotel had carpark cameras or even a number-plate recognition system. Tanya will have to do without it until this is over, don't even tell her where it is. You choose the station."

He headed clockwise on the Third Ring Road, a good choice. These days it had had no traffic lights. I guessed we were headed for Ugreshskaya but he pulled off at the first exit and drove directly towards the city center.

"Dubrovka, Metro line 10. You used the MCC line last time, remember."

"Clever boy. Maybe you are not such a flatfoot after all. I was just thinking, how is your German these days?"

"Good, I have family there. But you knew that, right?"

"I read your file. Your father was stationed in Dresden before the wall came down?"

"Yep. And my mother is from Leipzig."

"You do the talking. We are German businessmen. Luggage lost at Sheremetyevo Airport, inbound on Aeroflot from Dresden. You know the drill."

"I do."

He took his hand off the wheel and looked at his gold watch.

"The four thirty Aeroflot afternoon flight gets in around

eight, so best to check in around nine."

Smart, but I hope he isn't getting too smart for his own good. Cocky just now could get us both killed, but I can't be too hard on him, he is a rookie.

"Good thinking. That gives us time to do our shopping and get a meal. After that I need a real drink."

We hit a couple of flashy foreign stores. Not surprisingly Kirilov had known where to shop. His choice of the Gum arcade, within a stones-throw of the Kremlin, had spooked me a little. But I guess they won't think to search here for us, we wouldn't dare.

Some of the sales staff in the high-end shops spoke passable German, much better than I could keep up with anyway. In an apparently American brand clothing store, which I had never heard of, he exasperatedly explained to the sales assistant about our lost luggage. Her German was good. As we dressed, she probably thought nothing from the other side of the curtain, of us wanting to change into the new clean clothes we had just bought. I hadn't showered and for once I hoped I smelt like it. We put our old clothes in the spare sports bag and emerged as 'Western' as we could. He carried it off better than me.

Over pre-dinner drinks Kirilov, getting into character, angled to stay at the Four Seasons hotel around the corner but I told him bluntly that this was too flashy to be wise. Besides, we only had a five-thousand-dollar budget and it would be best to pay cash. We settled on the lower profile Hotel National on Mokhovaya Street, just a short walk towards the Kremlin, and a quarter the price of the Four Seasons.

My steak arrived before his chicken salad. He nodded for

me to start and I didn't need asking twice. As the waiter retreated Kirilov leaned over and lowered his voice.

"So, we have three addresses to look into."

I slurped my wine to help down an ambitious first go at the overcooked steak.

"Three addresses for me to look into. I want you to check there is nothing in the other cases, to make sure we haven't overlooked anything. And you have to be very careful. We can't afford to be setting alarm bells off all over the place."

He tried to hide his disappointment.

"OK, I will use only my local police contacts. To be fair from what I remember most of these cases probably made the local papers at least, so I will start with that for background."

"Who are you thinking of in the cops?"

"I have a new friend who is a sergeant in the First Operational Regiment, mounted. He was the first officer in attendance at a nasty crime scene in an early case I was assigned. He is at their HQ on Viktorenko Street, by the Airport Metro. A handy place for us and he owes me a favor. He was drunk when he showed up at the scene, but he is a good guy, so I covered for him in my official report."

"Sounds good. While you do that, I will try the city library and research those addresses."

A waitress came over with an enormous chicken salad on an oversized plate. Conversation over.

With a plan in place I ordered another bottle of wine. I needed to switch off. The close shave with the SVR at the hotel had rattled me. After dinner I made good use of the bar, while he paced himself. That was how it worked in the old KGB tradition. Kirilov, as the junior officer, could enjoy himself up to a point but was ultimately responsible for his superior's wellbeing, especially when drinking. Security agencies come and go, are named and renamed, but the traditions endure.

A second bottle of wine and two cocktails to the good, he helped me into a taxi. Just after nine and we headed for the Hotel National.

At reception he propped me up on a sofa leaning against a pillar. I could hear him recounting our lost luggage story in his impeccable German from across the lobby. Explaining that I was the boss and had dealt with a very frustrating days travel a little excessively at the airport bar, he needed to get me to bed quick. Tomorrow was a big day for us. Aeroflot had apparently promised our luggage would be delivered to the hotel overnight.

Taking pity on him the attractive receptionist allowed him to pay for one night in cash. Before she handed over the room keys, she made him swear on his mother's grave to check in properly and register a company credit card in the morning. The charming German businessman took the oath and threw in his grandmother's grave for good measure.

Kirilov yanked me up and guided me to the elevator. Minutes later he pushed me onto the bed and removed my slip-on shoes. There was no way he was going to undress me. My new suit would just have to cope.

I mumbled a goodnight before I was out of it. Soon in my

deepest and best sleep for weeks, dreaming of dachas, notebooks, Kislitsyn, German cars and money, lots and lots of money.

8 ALARM BELLS

September 24

We started early despite my thumping headache. I began by taking photographs of each page of all three notebooks, two photographs of each page.

I gave Kirilov the job of getting the photographs developed at a city center photo shop we used from time to time for rush jobs. They were expensive but discreet. I wanted one copy of the notebooks for the prosecutor and a backup copy for us. There would be no digital copy made. Despite his best efforts to convince me thumb drive copies would be safe I didn't really understand the limits of FSB or SVR electronic snooping. I wouldn't risk it.

The envelope I handed him was addressed to Sergei in the Crimea.

I mentioned it included instructions to hand deliver the contents to Prosecutor Litvanov in Moscow should we meet with an unfortunate accident. Sergei would find an alternative if Litvanov was similarly luckless. The case couldn't die with us. I needed to believe that.

I sent him on his way and left it a few minutes before following. I called the prosecutor from a pay-phone in a neighboring hotel lobby and arranged to meet that afternoon using the clumsy coded language we had agreed.

"*Dobroye utro*, Mr Litvanov? Your dry cleaning is ready."

"Can I collect it this afternoon?"

"Yes Sir, that will be fine, any time after two. Don't forget your receipt."

Meaning, meet you in the park at four, and don't forget to leave a chalk mark on the bench if it is safe to meet.

I spent the next few hours on the Metro, changing five times to complete what was in normal circumstances a twenty minutes journey. I still wasn't sure it was enough. I thought I recognized a man from an earlier train, he had a distinctive walk, but I wasn't sure and later when I looked back, he was gone. I could only wonder if he thought he may have been blown and had switched with someone else. If they had a big enough team, you never really knew.

The public library looked tired. It's not that things were better in Soviet days, when fortunes went on military spending as civilian infrastructure crumbled, but now with huge stolen fortunes lining the oligarchs' pockets and the libraries, workers apartments and pensions still no better, it felt worse.

At least some of the Communists believed they were doing the right thing for the people. Kislitsyn always thought that. A rotten apple like Stalin was never enough to spoil the Communist barrel for him, however much of a monster that Georgian peasant had been. My old friend had been a true believer.

The Gosudarstvennaya library was my first choice, as I knew for certain it would have everything I needed and after that brush with the SVR, I wanted a library in the suburbs.

To my surprise the stern looking lady at the front desk was not only helpful but friendly. She even showed me how to log on to the computers. Weighing me up when I arrived, she had correctly decided I was not among the computer literate. She showed me how to use the Yandex search engine and then spent some time showing me what were apparently new features in the latest release. Although I was more than glad for her help, I was relieved when she eventually said she had to get back. I wanted to get on with it.

There were computers along two walls of the reading room. One on the right was free, with only some self-absorbed kid at the other end, earphones in, oblivious to the outside world. Perfect, he would pay me no mind.

Inserting the thumb drive Kirilov had given me three folders appeared, one for each address. I carefully typed the first into the browser.

The first hit was 'Moscow European and International Property':

MANOR COMPLEX ON RUBLEVKA
7,800 square meters
POA

I clicked on this and it took me to a link for the downtown office of the company. There was a button to expand the properties displayed from fifteen to thirty or forty. I selected the maximum.

Two addresses among the list instantly grabbed my attention:

Rubin Estate
$1,066,293

COTTAGE VILLAGE LETOVO
$2,000,000

It took me a second or two to process. All three of the addresses noted by Kislitsyn for sale by the same agent, albeit a high profile international one. I was no property expert but all my instincts told me this was a lead, a cast-iron, solid, line of inquiry. Despite the danger we were in I felt a surge of relief, our investigation wasn't over, I hadn't failed my friend.

Heart racing, I looked around, searching for eyes on me and making no attempt to disguise it. Nobody was paying me the slightest attention.

I clicked on each property in turn. Under the 'Marketed By' details at the bottom of the webpage they listed their sales representative. Three times in a row I read the same name, 'Mikhail Balenkov'. Now the lead had become a man. Someone we could investigate, follow, interview, even arrest. We could get him to talk and we would get him to talk, whatever it took.

When I hovered the cursor over 'Balenkov' I found it was a live link. Clicking on it revealed a picture of a jolly looking fat man in a gaudy blue checked suit. Jeez, not even Kirilov would wear that. Instinctively I copied down the contact details into my battered pocket address book.

There was no one near the printer at end of the row, so I risked it and printed Balenkov's picture along with the individual property pages. I just about remembered what Kirilov had shown me and managed, after a couple of attempts, to delete the browser history and clear the cache memory. That done, I put my baseball cap back on and hardly slowing grabbed the pages off the printer as the last one spewed out.

Folding them carefully in half so nothing was showing I turned away from the CCTV camera by the entrance and waved the papers at the librarian who had helped me, before straightening and heading for the exit. I hoped to appear a satisfied customer rather than a shady character attempting to avoid surveillance. At least the librarian seemed to buy it. She smiled and waved back. I probably made her day.

Outside I breathed deeply and tried to clear my head and calm my thoughts. First and foremost, we had a link between the addresses that I could look into right away. Looking at my watch I thought there would be time to go to the city land registry before my meeting with the prosecutor. Even if that didn't pan out, I had a solid lead to tell Litvanov about. I had Balenkov, Mikhail Balenkov.

I was tempted to make straight for my new target's office, grab him by the throat and scream at him, just what was so special about these fucking mansions that cost Kislitsyn his life? He was the key to finding out, and I needed to know. But I also knew I couldn't risk everything by showing my hand and picking him up.

This one I had to play safe and play long. Much as I

wanted the short-term satisfaction of hanging him upside down and beating out of him who he was selling these properties for, and why, I couldn't.

I heard Kislitsyn's voice in my head, telling me to take one step at a time, calmly, thoroughly, thoughtfully. From the beginning he would counsel you to only pick the target up when you already knew almost all the answers to the questions you were going to ask them. Make them think you knew everything, then they may tell you something important you didn't know. Damn it, hour by hour, day by day, case by case I was becoming him. I knew that was the right approach now and what I would be ordering my younger colleague to do shortly.

I was getting tired. Much as I should do the whole anti-surveillance routine, I just didn't have the energy. I hailed a taxi, barking the street address of the Moscow land registry at a driver who looked like he had just pulled a double shift. He called in with the dispatcher, opened a window and lit a cigarette. Taking his cue, I did likewise, dragging heavily on mine. He looked exhausted and was in no state to go any faster so I sat back, listened to the music and tried to enjoy my smoke, doing everything I could to avoid thinking about a tail.

The land registry was older than the library and had even more of an official government building feel about it. It smelled of the kind of bleach that reminds you of a hospital ward.

I decided on a direct approach. I couldn't risk making enquiries but not finding out what I needed. I walked to the head of the line and showed the man at the desk my FSB credentials. He couldn't hide his disapproval at the interruption. Tough, I spoke loudly.

"I need to speak to a land registry researcher in private, right now."

Deadpan he dialed a three-digit number on the relic of a touch-tone phone on the desk.

"Nadya, come to reception to assist with a government official who obviously needs some help."

Ignoring his sarcasm, I didn't have to wait in silence long before I heard the buzz and clunk an electromagnetic lock release. Someone, presumably Nadya, appeared and held the door open for me. Her warm smile and good looks were in sharp contrast to the man at the front desk, who blended in nicely with the drab surroundings.

I followed her to a room behind reception. It had reinforced glass windows overlooking the front desk. This Soviet-era construction was like a prison, from a time when there was no question that a line for land registry documents needed to be monitored round the clock for anti-social elements or foreign spies.

"How can I help you?"

"If I give you a couple of property addresses can you tell me who owns them or the land they are built on?"

"Of course. Current owners I can look up online. For properties in the city limits I can check hardcopy records for owners going back for up to a hundred years or so, the files are all here, although that may take me a few minutes."

"They are all in the city. I can write the addresses down for you. Please be as quick as you can, this is a matter of national security."

I regretted saying it straight away. Eyes fixed on me she turned a page then handed me a notepad and pen.

I wrote down the three addresses from memory. She looked at what I had written down, not seeming put out.

"This shouldn't be a problem. I'll see what we have. I won't be long."

Nadya swiped the ID card hanging from the lanyard around her athletic neck and disappeared through a door on the opposite side of the observation room. I sat down to wait, thinking better of ignoring the imposing 'No Smoking' sign. With nothing else to do I inspected the line out front, luckily for me.

She kept her promise and just a few minutes later I saw her come through another doorway at the side of the main reception area. She had some papers in her hand and went straight to the front desk to talk to my happy friend. He inspected the papers closely.

He didn't once look up in my direction, which I was thinking would have been the natural thing to do when he knew I was there and clearly thought I was a pain in the ass. He picked up the phone on his desk and dialed what was obviously a longer than three-digit internal extension number. An outside line. Alarm bells rang loud and clear in my head. I had to be quick.

As Nadya came back into the waiting room I made my move.

"Damn, there was another address I forgot to mention. It's just come to me and it needs checking urgently too, sorry."

She maintained her cool.

"No problem, I can check that one for you as well."

Nadya's thin smile looked forced.

"I can write the address down for you again. Here give me those."

I took the papers off her so she could open her notebook and get the pen from the front pocket of her coat.

I made up an address in an area near one of the three I had given her. Closing her notebook, she motioned for the papers she had given me.

"Oh, don't worry, I will hang on to these until you get back".

She paused but thought better of doing anything she might regret. Now all manners, I stepped forward to hold the door after she had swiped her ID to enter the registry. As she rushed off, likely straight back to reception, I slowed the closing door making sure the magnetic lock was not engaged. I could hear her quick footsteps heading away along the uncarpeted corridor, waiting until I guessed she had turned a corner.

The wail of the alarm shattered the calm of the registry. This time the man on the desk looked straight at me, then turned back to the front door, no doubt willing that arrival of the police.

I slung the registry door wide open, happy for it slam behind me. Not wanting to confront a returning Nadya, especially if she had gathered help, I turned in the opposite direction she had taken and ran. As I rounded the corner, I could see an illuminated "Fire Exit" sign at the far end of a dim corridor, lights flickering into life behind me. There was no one there to stop me. Running the full length of the corridor I burst through the emergency door, into the daylight.

Police cars shot by, screeching around the corner toward the front entrance. I stuffed my baseball cap on and walked away from the commotion, forcing myself not to break into a giveaway run.

Think, man think.

Right, if I stick to buses, I will still have enough time to make my meeting with Litvanov. I removed my coat, mingling with those at the first bus stop I came to. I already had enough to brief him, with the Balenkov lead, but as I folded the records from the registry and put them carefully in my inside coat pocket, I hoped they would give me more.

9 PRAYERS

Settling on to the back seat of the half empty bus, after no more than a cursory check on the passengers, I unfolded the land registry documents. They were microfiche copies of what looked like World War One era records.

Each of the pages seemed to be a separate record of a plot of land, rather than a street address. The text was blurred, but I could more easily make out what seemed a more recent official stamp next to where it said 'Owner'. The accompanying signature on all three documents was familiar to me, though I could hardly believe what I read. The stamp was in bold:

"*Komitet Gosudarstvennoy Bezopasnosti*, KGB, Committee for State Security".

All three plots had belonged to the KGB. And I recognized the original signature on the documents. Felix Edmundovich Dzerzhinsky, the first Director of Lenin's secret police, the Cheka, forerunner of the KGB. It looked like a KGB stamp had been added later to make it crystal clear who retained ownership, not that anyone would be stupid enough to ask for clarity.

I looked at the stamps again, as if I could have made a mistake recognizing the KGB sword and shield. The same KGB I had joined. The KGB that eventually became the FSB and the SVR when it was divided up as Communism fell, supposedly as a check on the spy agencies in a post-Soviet Russia.

That was before the rise to the top of ex-KGB Major Vladimir Vladimirovich Putin, which put the Russian Intelligence Services right back at the very center of power in the new Russian Federation.

I pushed open the narrow bus window. I suddenly needed air. The KGB had owned the land that all three houses Kislitsyn was interested in had been built on. He had made a point of inquiring about them with Gerzkov but didn't share with him why. I let that sink in. Presumably the FSB or the SVR, or both, had inherited the land. Had they kept the land and built the houses or had someone taken it? Who had lived there? Who had profited? What did Kislitsyn find out that got him killed? Question after question came to mind, each as shocking as the last.

Turning my head to the window I forced my breathing, slower and deeper, just as Kirilov had showed me the last time he thought I was having a panic attack.

I was relieved that I was on my way to share the burden with Litvanov. No, not to share the burden, that was not quite it. I needed someone to tell me what to do next, to give me orders. That's what I need now, that's what I was used to. I needed Kislitsyn. I felt exhausted, totally spent and utterly useless.

Staring out of the window, not on anything in particular, I let the blurred images occupy me, an impressionist landscape of hedges, trees, buildings, cars and people came in and out of focus.

It was with a start that I realized we were at the park bus stop. People were taking their seats. I bolted out of the rear door just as it began to close. Litvanov, God, someone, help me.

Entering through a side entrance I breathed a sigh of relief when I spotted the prosecutor's chalk mark on the bench. Between the trees I caught sight of him feeding the ducks. He looked an ordinary, carefree, old man relaxing on his way home from the office. He glanced in my direction and I knew I had caught his eye. Emptying his bag of dried bread, he brought the competing birds to a noisier frenzy, then turned and headed for a nearby bench. By the time I got there he had closed his eyes. I sat on the opposite end and opened the newspaper he had left for me.

"You don't look good Alexander. You need to look after yourself."

I was too tired for small talk.

"I am getting somewhere. You were right to be cautious."

"*Kto eto*? Who is it?"

"I don't have all the answers yet. I will get Kirilov to leave a full written report of what we have for you over the next few days. But the bottom line is Kislitsyn stumbled across or was tipped off about three properties up for sale. He had started keeping personal notebooks…"

"Kislitsyn?"

Litvanov knew him well. He was as surprised as I had been.

"I know, not at all like him. Anyhow, I managed to recover the notebooks he had taken to writing, it's not important how, but they were mainly old case notes of little interest. But in one I found a list in English of three addresses right here in Moscow. I found out they are all valuable properties and all currently for sale on an international real estate website by the same sales agent, a man called Mikhail Balenkov."

"Never heard of him."

"Me neither. But just before meeting you I went to the land registry to try and find out who owns the property or had previously owned it. I don't know about the houses, but all three plots of land were registered way back as owned by the KGB."

"*Der'mo*! shit!"

We fell quiet. I lit cigarettes for both of us.

He spoke first.

"Anything else? Tell me everything."

"Yes. The researcher at the land registry went straight to her supervisor before handing me the records. He made a call right away. Within minutes the Moscow Police were screaming down the street. I am surmising, but it looks like there were instructions in the files to report any inquiries about them. I was lucky to get away. Before that, I think some SVR or FSB goons turned up at our hotel. I don't know if they were looking for Kirilov and me specifically, but we didn't hang around to find out."

He took a long drag on his cigarette.

"I see. But I don't understand."

"What do you mean?"

"Sad though it is, it is not unheard of for senior members of the security or intelligence services to assume personal ownership of property they, shall we say, came into during the Soviet era and after a not too embarrassingly short gap sell it on for personal gain. We have had dozens of cases like this, but where our political masters have advised pursuing a prosecution was not 'in the interests of the state.'

"I guess. And your point is?"

"If Kislitsyn was murdered for this, and it seems standing orders left in place to apprehend anyone asking difficult questions about these houses, then there has to be more to it than that. As far as I know, none of the other cases of this kind of profiteering, even ones that we were able to prosecute, have ended up in murder."

I dragged long on my cigarette and thought about what he had said. He had a point.

"OK, so there must be more to it. To be honest without the land registry incident I would have thought I was simply on the wrong track and maybe even concluded the goons who showed up at the hotel weren't after us. But taken together, it must be something to do with the FSB or SVR taking an interest in Kislitsyn's investigation into those houses, agreed?"

"Yes."

"So, what do you want me to do now?"

Litvanov fell silent again. For a moment he seemed occupied watching the ducks.

"Concentrate everything on Balenkov. He is the link between the properties. Surely, he must know who he is working for and who will profit from selling them. That is what we need to know, before we can figure out what this is about and what got your friend killed."

"Follow the money?"

"Follow the money."

I had my marching orders. I stood up to go, but Litvanov grabbed my arm.

"Alexander, I don't like this. I want to be kept in the loop every step of the way. Does a meeting here, say once a week work for you?"

"I can make it work. And while we're at it, let's agree a new crash meeting code, just in case."

We both knew we would need it.

"What do you suggest?"

"I will call you on your cell phone and shout about a late case. I will give my name as Pakhomov. We will meet here exactly two hours after you receive that call."

"Got it. Remember Alexander go carefully and report in

with everything important. Use the crash code if you are contemplating taking any risky steps, before you take them."

I smiled.

"*Konechno*. Of course, would I do anything else?"

I am not sure whether Litvanov believed me one little bit.

Leaving the park by an exit on the opposite side, to a different bus stop, I wondered whether I should warn anyone. Mechanically I boarded the first that arrived. If they were looking for us at the hotel and if they had followed up with serious inquiries at the land registry, they will have checked the security cameras and identified me by now. They would know I wasn't on holiday in Crimea for a start.

I weighed up my options, knowing I had already put friends in danger and further contact from me now would be risky. Even so, I had to warn them, all of them, starting with the locals, the caretaker and the archivist. Then it dawned on me. My watchers can't have known about the notebooks. They had no idea how I knew about the three properties. Jesus, that massively increased the chances of Elena and Gerzkov getting picked up. They would be desperate to find out how I knew. I had to warn them, now.

I leapt up and rang the bell not caring where the next stop was.

"Stop, stop the bus".

The driver probably thought I was a drunk or a lunatic. Either way when he opened the door to be rid of me, I jumped off and ran down the street until I found a public phone. There was no way I was using the burner phone and maybe further pulling them into some perceived conspiracy against the state. Besides the old ways were best with Elena. She didn't trust phone conversations, as she said, you never knew who was listening.

I dialed her number from the payphone. When she answered I put the receiver down without saying a word. I immediately called her back. I let the phone ring five times then put the receiver down again. Elena knew better than to answer a second time. She would never forget her crash code, two hours after the number of rings, at St. Catherine's church. It was her church. A fallback was set at the same place every two hours. Without doubt, Elena would be there at seven. And she would warn Gerzkov for me when I asked her.

That left Sergei in Crimea. He was an old pro and if anyone wanted to play hardball with him, good luck to them. I didn't fancy their chances. Even so I decided to call him to tell him to stay cautious and, for what it's worth, to lay a little more smoke too.

"Hello."

"It's me. I have to be quick, no time for conversation."

Sergei took the cue and said nothing.

"Take a card and enjoy a few days away with the family. I think a trip abroad would be good for you too."

"Got it."

"Moscow rules."

He put the phone down without saying anything else. He had gotten the message.

*　　　*　　　*

St. Catherine's may be an unremarkable Moscow neighborhood church, but it was Elena's and special to her. She had always gone there, as far back as I could remember.

She was a remarkable woman, one of few I knew who could reconcile their Communist and Church orthodoxy, in her case seemingly without effort.

I was a few minutes early but she was already there. I sat beside her. There was nobody else nearby. She looked frightened.

"Alexander what is it?"

There was no point being guarded.

"I don't know the whole story but I don't like it one bit. Kislitsyn may have been murdered. That is what Litvanov the prosecutor has me looking into, why I came to see you the other day."

She stared at the altar, crossing herself, but said nothing.

"I am not sure, but I have a feeling someone has been following me, from time to time. Don't worry, I have made sure I am black now. But I need you to warn Gerzkov. I spoke to him about something with Kislitsyn and I am scared that if I see him in person again, I will put him in danger."

"What did you discuss with Gerzkov?"

"I am not going to tell you. I don't want you to know. It is safer this way. And don't ask him, that is an order."

I was not beyond pulling rank on my agents, even ones as old as Elena. Now she looked terrified. I softened my voice.

"Look it may be nothing, it's just a precaution but you know me. The older I get, the more cautious I become, just like the Major himself. Tell Gerzkov to take a few days and take that trip to the Baltic he was always talking about. A bit of sea air will do him good. Give him this."

I slipped a few hundred US Dollars into a bible on the back of the pew in front. Elena knew well enough not to touch it until I had gone.

"*Beregi sebya*, take care, Elena."

I left the church without looking back, hoping her mumbled prayers would provide some comfort, picturing her look of raw terror.

10 RABBIT

September 25

That morning I was driving. Kirilov had called the phone number on the real estate website and made an appointment to view one of the properties with Balenkov. We had picked the most expensive one.

He was to pose as a visiting representative of an independently wealthy and discreet German who was looking to develop business ties in Moscow. We decided on the most impressive address to announce his credentials. Kirilov had played his part to the full, telling the increasingly attentive secretary who answered, that he had no specific budget ceiling. Next, we hired a nondescript car, a Romanian Dacia, locally and for cash.

I parked two streets away from their office. It would be too risky for me to turn up and start asking questions but the chance that anyone would right now be able to connect Kirilov to me or the incident at the land registry was low. The plan was for Kirilov to only have one meeting with Balenkov and then break contact. The risk he would be identified was negligible. Despite this I remained nervous, reminded of the popular military maxim, 'the first casualty of any battle is the plan'.

"Remember, play it cool. Don't appear too keen or push too hard for information. Ask no direct questions about ownership whatsoever, a cautious representative, of an even more discreet German businessman. We might expect Balenkov to play his cards close to his chest but he is, after all, a salesman. He will talk, he won't be able to help himself. A hint that your boss would want to be very careful about the reputation of whoever he was buying from, that will be enough."

"Got it boss, a picture of discretion."

"And just confirmation Balenkov actually knows who the seller is, that is enough for now."

"Relax, I got it."

I understood Kirilov's short reply, I had said too much. We had already gone over and over everything as we drove. Cover story, exit strategy, different scenarios, the works. I needed to trust him to do his job. To be fair he looked the part in the new suit and sunglasses he had bought with my hard-earned dollars. He exuded confidence and as he was supposed to be representing a big shot foreign buyer, that was spot on.

"I will be watching every moment. After the meeting get Balenkov to drop you at the station. I will check for a tail on you and then stick with Balenkov to see what he does. I will text as soon as I have Balenkov appearing settled somewhere."

Kirilov was already opening the car door.

"No problem" he managed through a broad smile.

Jesus, he was enjoying himself. Thrilled by the chase and eager to get on with it. That used to be me twenty years ago. Not now, I had seen too many leave with a similar grin and not return.

He strolled off. I gave it a few minutes and followed.

I couldn't find a good observation point which irked me. From across the street I couldn't see into the ground floor real estate office at all. I was relieved to see that there were a few cars parked directly in front of the office, the one nearest the door a brand-new Mercedes. My gut told me it was Balenkov's. I kept my fingers crossed that there wasn't a back way out of the building to another car park.

The minutes ticked by. Each one seemed an age. The image that came to mind, over and over, was a repeat of the land registry incident. This time a picture of police cars hurtling up from nowhere as soon as Kirilov asked about that one particular address, not smiling, as he was bundled out of the office into an unmarked van.

Before I had time to let my imagination run even further away with me, a large fat man appeared in the office doorway and held the door open for a trim younger man wearing sunglasses. I had checked the local routes last night and I knew the likely ways they would go to view the house, so no need to run for the car. Mid-morning traffic was light, so I should have no trouble picking the Mercedes out.

As I crossed the street, I noticed Balenkov had still not

pulled out of the car park and forced his way across the road. Was he nervous, or just looking to avoid a bump in his spotless new Merc? Not too cautious I prayed, enough of a risk taker to trade a little sensitive information to get a big deal going.

I picked them up less than a minute or two later at traffic lights. Pulling in behind, I kept my distance, happy to see that nobody else was showing any particular interest.

Two turns later, after constantly scanning my mirrors, I allowed myself to believe there was no one close on my tail. I sat back and relaxed a little, opening the car window to enjoy a sunny drive in the countryside.

Balenkov pulled up to the gates, opening them with a remote control. The Mercedes cruised onto the drive, gates closing automatically behind, one at a time. The house was barely visible through the trees and shrubs. There was nothing I could do but wait.

I didn't want to be stuck in the car on such a beautiful day. Besides, if I stayed put, I may attract unwanted attention. The impressive row of mansions no doubt had their own private security guards to keep the likes of me at bay.

The bus stop and bench seat on the opposite side of the road looked promising, and seemed to have a line of sight to the drive. I crossed over, sat down in the sunshine and lit a cigarette in readiness for the wait. It was that time of year when you savored every moment in the sun, a desperate attempt to put off thoughts of the impending, seemingly endless, Moscow winter.

Three buses came and went. Nobody paid me much attention. The stop had two route numbers on it, so I suppose everyone on one bus assumed I was waiting for one on the other route. I looked at my watch again. Christ, Kirilov must be living up to his role. Taking a last drag I threw the butt down and stubbed it out with my foot. As soon as I straightened up the gates started to open.

I walked a little more quickly across the street, weaving between the traffic. It took all my willpower not to look directly at the Mercedes as it passed in front of me, fearing some stupid attempt at a signal from Kirilov.

Revving the engine, I pulled out quickly without signaling. Horns blasted. All my focus was on keeping contact with them as I wasn't sure which station Balenkov would go for. Damn, I should have thought of that yesterday and told Kirilov to pick one and stick to it. My heart was in my mouth when the Merc turned left through a gap in the traffic, just as I got stopped at a light.

Thirty-seconds more and I would have lost them. As the lights changed, I screeched off, happy the Dacia had more punch under the bonnet than I expected. I cut through the building traffic until I caught up with them. This time I got closer. Without any backup I couldn't risk getting stuck again.

I could see them chatting away, oblivious. Pulling up right outside the station, Balenkov got out of the car to shake Kirilov's hand, which I took as a sign 'the deal' was going well. Having spotted no tail, I followed Balenkov, almost all the way back to his office before my phone buzzed. A text message from Kirilov:

'He knows
Seller based Cyprus
He is not too smart'

Instantly my mind was racing. Cyprus, now that would be

a challenge. There was a lot of Russian mob money circulating there these days. A covert FSB investigation in Cyprus would be straightforward, they had a lot of friends there and many were expats they could call on for a favor. Few said no, and those that did had a habit of getting arrested or having an unfortunate accident. But this was completely different. What could Kirilov and I do there on our own?

My daydreaming was interrupted as Balenkov swung his car off the road, a roadside restaurant I hadn't seen coming. Too close to him, I carried on by and eased into the neighboring car park, a twenty-four-hour gym with plenty of parked vehicles to hide among.

Jumping out I walked back toward the restaurant, shielded by trees and a wire fence with big advertisements showing pictures of overly muscled men and women.

I wouldn't have to get too close. I could already see Balenkov sat at an outside table. Looks like he had the same idea to enjoy what could be the last of the sunshine that I had watching them back at the house.

He must be a regular, the waiter coming straight over to pour his wine before he had time to order. I guess when he thought he had a big sale he treated himself to lunch. We would be here a while. I sent a text to Kirilov and told him to change into jeans and a sweatshirt and get a taxi direct to the gym. I could debrief him in the car, well out of sight.

I settled against a tree watching Balenkov finish off his first two courses. I thought about Cyprus again. I personally had no friends there and couldn't think of anyone I could trust who had. I could always get someone like Sergei to travel there for me and ask a few questions, but without help from local law enforcement, why would anyone answer them? I knew Cyprus was a tax haven of sorts and from experience I knew that meant public records would be opaque at best, if you could find them at all. Moreover, the locals who knew anything, knew enough to keep quiet. My phone buzzed. Kirilov had arrived.

He sat in the back, slouching down to make it hard for anyone to pick him out from a distance. I got in the driver's side, still finishing my latest cigarette, opening a window before he had time to moan.

"Balenkov settled?"

"They were just serving dessert as you arrived. We have a few minutes."

He handed me his bag. Opening it I saw some leaflets with a cheesy picture of Balenkov and some information about his career and business interests.

"He is a lawyer from St. Petersburg, but now he acts purely in high-end real estate deals, no money in 'court law' he says."

St. Petersburg, so he was already with them.

"And he mentioned our sellers are in Cyprus?"

"I told him my German client did a lot of business across Europe, especially Southern Europe and the Mediterranean, and was looking to expand east. He then just offered up that information, I didn't have to push him at all."

In silence I quickly read through the blurb, then reread some of Kirilov's research. But I was conscious of the passing minutes.

"I'll go and keep eyes on the target. Stay here and put that baseball cap on. You can drive. I will wave you over when he makes a move."

When I got back to my tree, I could see he was in no rush. He spent another twenty minutes finishing. Not bothering to call the waiter back, he just weighed some notes down with the ashtray and got up to go. As I thought, a regular.

I stepped back through the gap in the trees and waved Kirilov over. As he pulled up, he leaned over and opened the passenger door before the car had come to a halt, as was his habit.

"I think he will head back to the office. Wait for him to pass us and pull out a couple of cars back. No need for you to get too close."

Kirilov did exactly as he was told. He was quiet, focusing on the Mercedes and keeping his distance. Suddenly, just as the main road straightened out before his office, Balenkov accelerated and without signaling pulled a fast, sharp, right onto a side street. As we zoomed after him, I saw why.

"*Der'mo*. They are here. And Balenkov has spotted them."

Two new BMW's had pulled up directly outside his office. One goon in a trademark dark suit and wrap-round sunglasses stood by each vehicle, guarding the scene from passersby.

"*Kto*? Who?"

I snapped back.

"Whoever killed Kislitsyn! Whoever is searching for us! Balenkov is bolting. Keep on him!"

Kirilov made the turn more smoothly, not wanting to attract any attention from the suits outside Balenkov's office. They had come for him. My stunt at the land registry had brought about a bigger reaction than I could have anticipated.

I must be right about them not knowing about Kislitsyn's notebooks. They must think I found out about the properties directly from Balenkov. And for him to bolt like that on first sight of them, he must believe that what he knows about whatever is behind this property deal is enough to put him in real physical danger.

"Step on the gas and keep him in sight. Maintain your distance though, he will be looking out for them. Now it begins, the rabbit is running. But where?"

11 OPERATION RYAN

September 25

My mind was in turmoil after Balenkov's shooting on the bridge. I had gone over everything from the first meeting with the prosecutor right up to the moment the gunman pulled the trigger. I had signed Balenkov's death warrant when I pulled those land records.

Kirilov said something but I missed it. He repeated his question.

"Where exactly is this apartment?"

For the first time the reality of who and what we were up against was beginning to tell on him.

"I think we were being followed. I saw two men in a van back there, focused on us not Balenkov. The apartment belongs to an old friend. We can't go back to the hotel, even to pick anything up. Aside from the computers did we leave anything that they could use?"

"Your old camera? But I have all the photographs of the notebooks in my bag, and the negatives. There is nothing saved on the computers, it's all on the thumb drives and I have them with me."

"Good, I have kept the original notebooks on me. And we still have a couple of thousand dollars."

I gave him directions to the apartment and we drove on in silence. He was getting to know me and I think he realized I needed some quiet to think.

"I am going to arrange a crash meeting with Litvanov to let him know about Balenkov."

This was no time to go rogue. We needed all the official cover we could get. Maybe the prosecutor could help us, maybe he could even protect us. He was our best shot anyway.

Kirilov dropped me off so I could loop around on foot and conduct at least a basic surveillance check, before he headed off to dump the rental car in an underground car park. I told him at least four blocks away from the apartment building would be wise.

As I walked, I racked my brain trying to think of anyone in the office would know of my friendship with Yuri, the holidaying apartment owner. I couldn't think of anyone. He was an old neighbor who worked as a flatfoot for the police.

His wife had been very good friends with Viktoriya, brought closer together by their distress at being unable to have children. I liked him and even after they had moved away, the four of us went for a meal every couple of months. We had never had anyone else dine with us and for the life of me I couldn't think why I would have mentioned these nights out to anyone at work other than Kislitsyn. I really didn't know anyone else there as a friend.

I looked under the doormat outside the flat for the key but he had moved it. I felt along the ledge above the door and there it was. Thank God for predictable and dependable cops like Yuri.

The apartment smelt a bit musty but was clean and tidy. More importantly it stood a chance of being safe, for the time being anyhow. I checked the blinds and curtains in every room, finding they were already closed. By then Kirilov was knocking on the front door.

"Car is five blocks back. I tailgated someone into an underground carpark and parked on the bottom level between a big four by four and a van. There was no one around and there were no cameras, so I pulled up right next to the barrier and switched our back plate with a clamped car a few spots down. It had been there for a while. It could buy us a couple of days."

"Good. Now I want you to get a shower, something to eat and some rest. God knows when we will next have time to do that. I am going to meet the prosecutor. I shouldn't be more than two hours. If I don't text you by then, run."

"Got it. And I smell that bad? Ok, but you are not exactly scented roses yourself."

The humor was forced. He already looked older than just a few short days ago. Balenkov's murder right in front of us had hit him hard.

"I'll shower later. And Kirilov, lock the door behind me."

I walked down a few streets and changed direction several times before even looking for a payphone. I didn't want to call from one too close to our latest so-called safe house. I felt nobody had been behind me and going in the same direction after the last few turns, so now was as good as ever. I found a payphone and dialed the prosecutor's number.

"Litvanov its Pakhomov. Have you got that case file done yet? I need to get started, immediately."

He disconnected the call without a word.

With accelerating events and the death of our main lead I just didn't have time to undertake a full anti-surveillance. I had no choice but to cut corners. We had to speed up or they would catch up with us before we got to the truth.

I took a taxi straight there and got the driver to pull up directly across from the park entrance. I threw some notes at the taxi driver and strode into the park.

A few minutes along the path I glanced round and spotted him a short way behind. I slowed down and continued clockwise around the perimeter path of the park, waiting for him to catch up.

"Alexander, there you are. Let's sit, I am a little out of breath."

I gestured towards an empty bench, with nobody on the ones either side. I sat close to him, so we didn't have to raise our voices. In just a few minutes I told him everything that had happened. He didn't say anything for a long time.

"Look I have had an idea. I must say it's a bit unusual and I think at first you will not like it at all, but Alexander, please just think about it for a moment. Promise me you will do that, consider it carefully."

"We are desperate, I will consider anything. Anyway, what could be so …"

"Let me tell you a story first. It's about Kislitsyn and it's why I have come to the decision I have."

He had shifted from agreeing strategy with me at our last meeting to telling me what he had decided we would do. I was glad.

"You may not know any of this, but back in the early Eighties when that madman Ronald Reagan was President, the KGB and GRU became concerned the US was actively planning a surprise nuclear attack against us. As a result of these concerns the KGB set in place a new top-secret full-scale intelligence collection program, known as *Raketno-Yadernoye Napadenie*, known to insiders as Operation RYaN."

"This I have heard of."

"It was set up to find out what US intentions were regarding a nuclear missile attack and how we could create a working early warning system to alert us when the West was making final preparations for a first strike. Kislitsyn was seconded to Operation RYaN."

"Kislitsyn?"

"You never knew? Anyway, Operation RYaN gained a momentum of its own over time, eventually spiraling out of control with the hawks in the Kremlin spinning its findings to argue the US was categorically on the warpath. It was the worst case of confirmation bias I have seen in your old department's work. Everything that supported the thesis of a mad sneak attack by Reagan was reported, and everything that suggested the alternative rejected as not relevant. We were actually on the verge of the lunacy of a preemptive Soviet nuclear attack to thwart what our Party leadership was being told, and believed, was a genuine US plan to strike first. Believe me Alexander, this was a far more dangerous moment in the Cold War than even the Cuban Missile Crisis, but unlike Cuba, back then the public knew nothing about it."

"OK, thanks for the history lesson, but what's this got to do with our problems right now?"

"I knew all about RYaN from the start. I have never discussed this with anyone apart from Kislitsyn before, it was ultra-secret, but he sent someone to London back then as an inside man on RYaN to report back to him everything that was going on. Even the Rezidentura didn't know Kislitsyn's man was there. They thought he was there to help the Ambassador. I know he had no contact with your people, or the GRU and he reported directly back to Kislitsyn. Now I know you were there at the same time and your mission to London was exclusively to work on RYaN and report back to Moscow, direct, again outside the Rezidentura."

"Interesting. I had no idea you knew anything about it or my time there."

"Kislitsyn sent his man over every few weeks when he wanted something specific. He kept away from the Embassy and Rezidentura people, and you?"

"I was tasked with collecting my own intelligence for RYaN, first hand, from my own hastily recruited and unwitting local sources. I was not allowed to rely on any existing KGB or GRU assets and I reported nothing to the Rezident. Everything was reported back direct to my RYaN handler in Moscow"

"Clever of Kislitsyn to recruit his own man for a parallel operation and check up on you."

"Do you know what Kislitsyn did with the information his man provided."

"That, he never shared with me. I know he thought the whole RYaN thing was dangerous political and military interference in the proper conduct of KGB operations."

"He promised me he would keep me out of politics. Just collect the RYaN material like I was tasked, but also let him know personally, exactly what I had sent back to Moscow."

"There he was a true friend to you. Of course, he did the opposite to what the Generals expected. He took the Kremlin hawks on at their own game. It was through the actions of Kislitsyn and a small group of like-minded KGB officers of similar rank, that a war of unimaginable horror was averted. Kislitsyn personally circumvented the Generals manipulating Operation RYaN intelligence by building a new secret back channel to the Reagan administration through the deputy CIA station chief here in Moscow."

"No fucking way. There is now way he could have..."

"Kislitsyn risked everything and gave advanced copies of your Operation RYaN reports directly to the CIA Moscow

Deputy Chief of Station, a man named Bradley Powell. For Kislitsyn treason charges and summary execution awaited if he were found out. But he wasn't, thank God."

"I can't believe it, him of all people, working with the Americans. Never in a million years would I have thought that. And only he could have got away with it, anybody else would have been caught."

"Through his reports the Americans, although skeptical at first, avoided the specific activities Operation RYaN agents like you had identified as actual triggers confirming US preparations to launch a preemptive strike. That was the kind of thing you were tasked to report back from London, right?"

"Exactly that, I was allowed to report only on a small range of very specific questions. Anything from increased troop movements to an increase in payment for blood donations. Unbelievably Moscow didn't even know the UK was different from the US and did not pay blood donors. I tried to tell them but was cut down. We were to report only facts against the specific questions tasked and were to provide no analysis or assessment, of any kind. It was utter madness."

"The hawks were totally mad. They were cunning too. But Kislitsyn and Powell, they were smarter. The American managed to get the US military to avoid the triggers, but not give Kislitsyn's help away, inventing cover stories for cancelled joint exercises with NATO and so on. In time the back-channel collaboration deescalated the crisis and avoided war. Simultaneously, other mid-ranking KGB officers, with better political connections than Kislitsyn, exposed the collusion between the Operation RYaN Generals and the Kremlin hawks to the Party leadership."

"Jesus. That's some story. But if I remember right, back then, when I was in England, Kislitsyn was supposed to be helping the STASI with trouble in Berlin. All the time he was here, in Russia working to undermine RYaN?"

"Operation RYaN was beyond top secret, very few people outside the operation knew anything whatsoever about it. And Kislitsyn was not in Russia all the time, he was everywhere."

"So how come you know all about it, including Kislitsyn's man in London and the back channel with the Americans?"

"He never told me much of this story. I was only fully read into RYaN after the event. The Party leadership launched a secret internal inquiry under a Special Prosecutor, prompted by Andrei Andreyevich Gromyko, which continued its investigations under Andropov. It has never been made public and never will be. I worked for the Special Prosecutor, but in a very junior capacity you understand. Even Kislitsyn wasn't fully briefed about the inquiry. We were all sworn to secrecy and we knew that meant on pain of death."

"Hell, that is some story. I would never have believed he could keep something so momentous secret from me, of all people, for all these years. Interesting, even amazing, but why are you telling me all this now? What has it got to do with Balenkov and Kislitsyn's murder?"

"Bradley Powell is back in Moscow. He is acting as a special military attaché at the US Embassy on behalf of the new Director of National Intelligence."

I only had to look in his eyes for a second to understand he was deadly serious.

"You can't be suggesting I go and ask the Americans of all people for help with this?"

"That's exactly what I am suggesting. Alexander, think about it. We both want to find out the truth about who murdered our friend. We know the only leads we have left point outside Russia, specifically to Cyprus. And we know the Russian Intelligence Services, or elements within them, are directly involved in the murders. There is nobody else we can we turn to."

Litvanov had a point.

"But why would Powell want to help us?"

"Powell was Kislitsyn's friend for years after the Operation RYaN crisis. The Party leadership, particularly Minister of Foreign Affairs, Andrei Andreyevich Gromyko, never fully trusted the Generals again, suspecting them all of being war-mongering hawks, of one stripe or another. Wary of another attempt by remaining hardliners in the military and security services to push the USSR into war, they encouraged Kislitsyn to keep his secret back channel with Powell open and report directly to them. The Party leaders knew the value of direct communication with the US intelligence community and through it with the White House. The channel remained open. RYaN wasn't the only flashpoint. Kislitsyn and Powell met on occasion and remained friends."

"Working with the Americans on this is very risky. I need some protection should the whole thing go south."

He didn't say anything. He didn't have to. There was no other option.

"I will do it but with two conditions. First, you give me official instructions, in writing, that this is how you ordered me to proceed with the investigation. Second, you provide a written immunity from prosecution for treason should this investigation be uncovered before it is completed."

"Agreed, I will have that for you at our next meeting. How do you plan on making covert contact with Powell?"

"We have to have our secrets too you know. You concentrate on the strategy and sorting legal cover and leave the spying to the professionals. Goodnight Litvanov, speak to you soon."

I got up, putting on a confident stride towards the exit for the prosecutor's benefit.

If he knew that my only thought was to walk straight through the front door of the US Embassy tomorrow and ask to see a security officer, he would probably have laughed out loud. But with no knowledge of Kislitsyn's back channel procedures, having never met Powell and with no contacts of my own in US intelligence, that was exactly what I planned to do.

12 EMBASSY

September 26

That morning I had thought about going to an internet café to do some research on Bradley Powell to prep for my approach. I decided against it as the land registry debacle and Balenkov's murder had me rattled, particularly my suspicion they were directly connected. Going to the US Embassy in person was plenty enough risk as it was. There was no need to show myself before then.

I shaved for the first time in days, leaving an unconvincing mustache. Kirilov laughed when he saw it. When I took his Hugo Boss sunglasses and his jacket off him to complete my 'disguise' he was less amused.

Putting him the picture about Litvanov's idea to approach the Americans I tried to avoid telling him the whole story. That didn't work. He was perplexed at the reasons behind the idea and horrified I would consider it. I was left with little choice but to tell him the Operation RYaN story to get his buy-in. I left out that I had previously known nothing about Kislitsyn's back channel or his other source in London. I wanted him to believe I had a far better understanding of events over time than I did. This was no time to undermine his confidence in me.

The US Embassy was on Bolshoy Devyatinsky Lane, in central Moscow, just a couple of miles east of the Kremlin. The rental car was off limits. I had any number of ways of getting there on public transport.

Russian security services monitored everyone going in and out of the Embassy. It would be better if Kirilov could go, but this fly by the seat of your pants mission was not for a newcomer. There were so many pitfalls and on the spot decisions to be made. It had to be me, despite my face being better known and recently captured by land registry surveillance cameras. The dodgy moustache and sunglasses would have to do. At least if the weather held up, I had an excuse for wearing them.

Going through the motions but also wanting to keep Kirilov busy I arranged to text him with a station I was headed to after a couple of switches on my way to the Embassy. He was to pick me up on foot there and look for anyone tailing me. I went through standard procedure for such tactics with him in detail, and we agreed three or four likely stations for me to aim for that he could get to easily. I had to admit this was as much for my benefit as his. This kind of routine procedure stuff occupied me, leaving less time for me to consider the myriad ways today could all go bad.

On the plus side there was no reason to suspect that anyone would have any inkling we would be seeking help in our investigation from the Americans. How would they put together Kislitsyn's role in Operation RYaN, Litvanov's connection with it, his out of the box idea to contact Powell or even that I was currently working at the prosecutor's direction? Moreover, neither Kirilov nor I had any recent contact with US liaison in Russia or elsewhere.

No, the risk was from routine monitoring of all people in and out of the US Embassy. With current tensions between Russia and America and another round of tit-for-tat expulsions of 'diplomats', my worry was that security on both sides would be heightened.

I had gone over and over my options in my head, such as they were. The best of a bad lot seemed to be a direct approach, purporting to be a US travel visa applicant. Once in the building, to then as discreetly as possible identify myself as a serving FSB officer to the front desk, seeking an immediate meeting with security, before my pitch to meet Powell. I hoped they had well-versed procedures for a 'walk-in'. God knows what would happen then, but hopefully they won't sling me out as a lunatic.

It was the technical FSB surveillance of the Embassy that I was most concerned about, CCTV and facial recognition software. This stuff was getting increasingly capable and I was not a hundred percent sure that a new moustache, sunglasses and baseball cap would do the trick. Would they already have my picture on a 'Red Alert', shared with FSB Counter Espionage officers at ports and monitoring embassies? It was a risk, but it was one we had little choice but to take.

Kirilov offered his hand. A little embarrassed I shook it. I guess it was his way of saying good luck without drawing attention to the obvious dangers. I gave him the notebooks.

"You may as well keep these. Remember the crash meeting protocol with the prosecutor. If I don't contact you within four hours of leaving here, arrange to meet Litvanov tonight. Take everything with you, including the notebooks, and give it all to him. What happens from then on is completely up to him."

"*Ya ponimayu*, I understand".

An hour later and I was walking from the bus stop towards Bolshoy Devyatinsky Lane. One modern building stood out. There was one police officer monitoring the line of people snaking towards it, comfortable inside a small temporary building, another open to the elements just beside the entrance. A CCTV camera stuck out from the hut roof, but of more concern, half of the front windows had tinted glass. The FSB man would be there, out of sight.

The old lady in front of me turned, smiling.

"We are going to see our daughter, Natasha, she married an American, in New York."

Appearing to be with them could lower the interest of police or FSB officers scanning the line with my mugshot. It was too good an opportunity to miss. Story time.

"Anatoli, I am going to America for a conference, just a work thing, not as exciting as your trip."

"Ludmilla, and this is my husband Gregor."

We exchanged pleasantries and I did my best to keep the small talk going. Ludmilla told me she had problems with what one or two of the questions on the visa paperwork meant. I asked her to show me. By the time we worked our way to the front of the line I had picked up Ludmilla's bag as she was pointing out questions she couldn't answer.

The three of us were too focused on the form to pay the policeman shepherding the line towards US territory too much attention. I hoped it was mutual. Just as I thought we were going to make it he held the line.

"What's the problem?" Ludmilla asked.

"It's no problem for us. We hold the line when the line on the US side extends out of their office."

I held my breath, focusing my gaze on the small print on the bottom of the form.

"OK."

That was all the police officer said. The three of us stepped over the line onto US territory and walked towards the door of the US security checkpoint. Ludmilla and Gregor were not quick on their feet and that was probably a blessing. I felt sure I would have broken into a run without them to slow me down.

Behind me I could hear raised voices as the officer had an issue with those next in line. Perfect timing. The door of the US checkpoint opened, a man in a private security uniform holding it, while I helped Gregor and Ludmilla up the step.

"You have to go through the security check first, a metal detector, just like at the airport. Please empty your pockets and remove phones, coins, belts, and any large metal items. Your bags will be searched. Do you understand?"

I replied in the affirmative, then told Ludmilla and Gregor what to do, as he'd explained they hadn't flown abroad for years. Reassuring Gregor that it would be fine and that I would keep an eye on it all the way, I put his watch and money in a little plastic tray on the conveyor belt. Neither of them had a phone.

I glanced up looking for what I needed. On the other side of the metal detector security contractors were using wands to complete the security checks. Just beyond them was a US Marine. He looked like a recruitment poster. I needed to speak to him, I desperately needed him to believe me.

I put my phone, wallet, keys, belt and coins in a plastic tray. The security guard behind the scanner took it from me and put it on the conveyor belt. I kept my FSB credentials hidden in my trouser pocket. I knew it would set the metal detector alarm off. That was how I would attract that Marine's attention.

As I stepped through the metal detector the alarm rang out. A security contractor with a wand moved over to search me. Making eye contact with him I opened my credentials so just he could see what they were and spoke softly.

"FSB, Russian Security Services. I need to talk to that Marine officer urgently, but quietly. Believe me, it is in all our interests that we do not cause a scene."

By now Ludmilla, Gregor and one or two security contract staff were staring in my direction.

The Security Contractor looked up at me and then back at my credentials, weighing up what to do. After what seemed an eternity, he handed them back, motioned me forward and walked toward the American serviceman.

"Sergeant, you need to speak to this man?"

My heart was pounding as the Marine stepped forward from his post, and addressed me, but I took a deep breath and stuck my chest out. I had to be assertive, I was here on FSB business.

"Sir?"

The contractor gestured for me to show the Marine my credentials.

He took no more than a glance at them. He knew what they were.

"What is it you want sir?"

"I need to see an Embassy security official immediately, but discreetly. It is a matter of great importance to both our countries."

The Marine nodded barely perceptibly to the security contractor, who handed him the plastic tray with my things.

"Follow me."

He marched forward with me in tow. As we passed his post the Marine corporal who had been on the opposite side of the gangway moved over, guarding the one access door to the Embassy itself.

I was in.

"This way."

The sergeant turned first left down a grey featureless corridor. Halfway down there were two doors on opposite sides, with a light over each, illuminating the word 'Unoccupied' in green, or "Occupied" in red.

He opened the door under one set of lights and gestured towards a chair. Along with a second chair and bare table there was no other furniture and there were no pictures. But there was a tall mirror, running the full length of the wall opposite the door. He kept the plastic tray and its contents.

"I will need your credentials. I won't keep them long."

I hesitated but handed them over. I wasn't used to parting with them, but in the circumstances, I had to.

"Wait here. No smoking."

I expected more questions but he was already headed out the door. Through the glass over the door I saw a red light come on, and almost simultaneously heard an electro-magnetic lock engage. I was going nowhere.

The small room was hot and the wait seemed an eternity. An hour, maybe. There was no clock and my phone and watch were with the Americans. God knows I could do with a cigarette. I would have risked ignoring the sergeant's instructions, but in my haste to get here I left my cigarettes in Yuri's apartment.

Then the door snapped open. A trim young man in a suit entered. The same sergeant waited outside, filling the doorway in case anyone had thoughts of storming in to get me.

The new guy placed my wallet, phone, watch and credentials on the table.

"Major Danilov, I am Stephen from the security section. How can I be of assistance?"

"I need your help. I need to speak urgently with Bradley Powell, today."

Stephen was not fazed, or if he was, he made no show of it. What you would expect from what I assume was a CIA officer, a professional and one chosen to serve in their main enemy's back yard.

"Is this request in an official or personal capacity?"

I think he was expecting me to say personal. This was not the normal way official contacts were made. Most likely he was wondering what I was selling, the latest of a line of traitors selling Russia's intelligence crown jewels for a quick buck.

"Let's just say it's in an official capacity, but not in an authorized one."

Now I had his attention. Maybe I was not another 'walk-in' or counter-espionage officer disingenuously offering the keys to the FSB castle in a ploy to entrap a US 'diplomat'.

"Can you explain what you mean by official but not authorized?"

"I could try, but nothing I will tell you now will make much sense to anyone, other than to Powell. I have a message from my former boss, Colonel Kislitsyn, for Mr. Powell. Only he will be able to fully understand it."

"Colonel Kislitsyn? The FSB Kislitsyn? He passed away, didn't he?"

Young Stephen knew his stuff. He was more than I could have hoped for.

"He did and he was murdered, as was another man here in Moscow yesterday. I think Bradley Powell is the only man who can help me find out why. I must speak to him personally, and every day's delay carries with it the risk of more bloodshed, and the risk we will never get to the bottom of the murders."

He continued to hold my gaze for an age, assessing me. Then he made to leave.

"Someone will meet you at the Church of Saint Nicholas, eight o'clock tonight. The 612 bus stops right outside. Take it and come alone."

"Will Powell be there?"

He knocked on the door which opened instantly, the serviceman stepping aside.

"I am not at liberty to say."

I knew he would tell me no more. He couldn't trust me, yet.

"Now, do you need a discreet exit from the Embassy?"

His rapid shift from skeptical diplomat to businesslike spy had caught me a little off guard.

"Yes, very discreet would be best for all of us."

"No problem, we'll get you out safely."

Five minutes later, wearing a new overcoat and wide-brimmed hat I was leaving with some of the Russian kitchen staff through a side door. The sergeant had arranged for a colleague in civvies to walk me to the corner, before leaving me there to make my own way. The man talked to me non-stop, in passable Russian, about the terrible price of food these days in Moscow. It seems his role was to keep any of the kitchen workers from getting too close and asking awkward questions. They kept their distance and in no time went their separate ways.

The man stopped talking mid-sentence.

"I leave you here."

He turned down a side street.

Suddenly I was very much alone.

13 POWELL

At the next corner I sent the prearranged text to Kirilov letting him know that I had been successful in arranging contact. I would follow up with the station name for his counter surveillance before I got there, but allowing just enough time for him to make it, full on Moscow Rules.

Scanning faces on my first leg, a short bus ride, it occurred to me that the Americans would have put a tail on me. It can't be every day that an FSB Major walks in unannounced and requests a crash meeting with a former CIA man, while making vague references to murder and a dead FSB senior officer. It was certainly possible they would want to see where I went that afternoon. Then again as they knew where to pick me up later, on the 612 to the church, they could start their surveillance then.

You idiot. There would be no US tail just now. They had kindly leant me an overcoat to help me sneak out. No doubt it would have some new high-tech tracker attached, a button or something in the lining. That would be the efficient way.

There was hardly any point in looking for it. And besides it gave me comfort that the Americans knew where I was. I could cling to the hope that if they had taken me seriously, they may even be interested in protecting me as a potential source.

It was a fair question, whether they took me seriously or not. A serving FSB officer who wandered in, asked for the CIA, spun a tale about a murdered colleague, provided no evidence but demanded to see an ex-Agency diplomat, now on a confidential mission to for the White House intelligence chief, because he was the only one who would understand. Would you take that seriously? Jeez, they probably think I am a trap, or a madman, maybe a both.

The bus bounced over a pothole bumping me off my seat, bringing me to my senses. Stick to the routine, concentrate on that. I made my first change at a stop with a bus already waiting on another route. No one else switched between the two buses. After just one stop I got off and made for a nearby Metro station. Again, nobody obvious making the same connection. Two trains and one taxi later I felt a little reassured that I hadn't seen anyone familiar from earlier.

I settled into a café for a bite to eat and to text Kirilov. Otradnoye District was in North Moscow, and the Metro Station there, on Line Nine, had trains running south every few minutes, so it was a good place to start my slow journey back to the church and my meeting with a perhaps retired senior American spy.

I ordered big. A ham and cheese *Blini*, and several *Pirozhki*, for which I had a particular weakness. I didn't know when I would get the chance for a proper meal again and I needed some energy to focus on this evening's challenges.

I tried to relax, but every time the café door opened, I couldn't help but look up to study the newcomers. I half expected men in dark suits, savoring the moment as they cornered their prey. The tension got to me and welcome as it was, I left before finishing, with a stomach too knotted to enjoy my food.

The entire time I was on the Metro I never caught sight of Kirilov. As I walked the last part of my journey to catch the bus, he texted:

'Clean. Good Luck.'

In my message back I told him to stay away from Yuri's apartment until I gave him the all clear after my meeting with Powell. I walked and sat in a park killing time, finishing one packet of cigarettes and buying another. They would be the death of me, maybe even before my enemies in the FSB got their shot.

At last it was time. Subconsciously I had gravitated in the right direction, eager to get started, with just a short walk left to the right bus stop. It was a quiet evening traveling south and as the arriving bus emptied only two middle-aged ladies got on with me. The driver read the paper as he waited for our scheduled departure time. As he readied to leave a short, stocky, man jumped on through the front doors as they were closing. He sat just a few seats behind the driver. I didn't place him from earlier today, but from where I was, I didn't have a good view. Although there was nothing that stood out about him, I was sure he was one of Powell's men checking on me and the other passengers, looking for signs of trouble, looking for signs I had backup.

There was little chance of making eye contact with anyone and spooking any of Powell's watchers. The two old women were complaining about their daughters, as if there was a prize for having the worst and the man in front had his head down, snoozing, or wanting it to look that way.

Not far from the church one of the old ladies got off, leaving three of us. I was glad that Powell's people didn't have too many people to rule out as FSB, ready and willing to swoop on a high-profile US spy, retired or not.

The 612 stopped right outside the church. I got off alone and waited for the bus to depart, pretending to check the timetable for a return journey. I surveyed the street before I turned and made my way up the church steps. I didn't see any suspicious looking vehicles parked anywhere too close to cause Powell to abort the meeting.

Saint Nicholas' church was in the classic Russian Orthodox style, its gilded domes perfectly in proportion. Show a picture of this church to virtually anyone, anywhere, ask them to guess which country it was from and most would guess correctly, first time. Saint Nicholas and churches like it had at times been the only refuge for Muscovites from the darker forces of State all the way back to the Romanovs. Like many in the past I needed such refuge just now. How ironic that it was to be provided here by Americans.

Entering through the heavy wooden front doors the church was dark, lit only by poor electric roof lights and the occasional flickering candle. My footsteps echoed loudly. A few women knelt praying near the altar. Further back there was a lone figure skulked in the shadows on a pew as far from the pious as you could get. It must be Powell or someone he had sent.

I made my way slowly, not wanting to startle anyone out of sight, choosing to sit on the row directly in front of him, that man I now recognized as Powell.

Although he must be more than seventy by my reckoning, he still carried a military bearing. Not quite the Marine poster boy from the Embassy yesterday, but not far off.

He spoke first. Good Russian, no doubt well used in his years as a spy chief here. He had even kept a trace of a Muscovite accent.

"Major Danilov, a pleasure."

"Alexander, please. Any friend of Kislitsyn, is a friend of mine."

"Alexander, then. What makes you believe I was a friend of Colonel Kislitsyn?"

This guy didn't hang around, all business. I liked that. He would expect no less from me.

"I know about Operation RYaN and the backchannel you and he ran from back then. Kislitsyn was my boss and a close personal friend for thirty years."

"Interesting. Nobody likes history more than me, but I am a busy man Major and my bosses would seriously disapprove if they knew I was here. What is it you think I can do for you, given I am a semi-retired diplomat after all, with no real influence here in Moscow these days? I am more of a PR man for the Pentagon types who don't like

Russian winters."

"Kislitsyn was murdered."

"Stephen briefed me. Perhaps I wouldn't be here if you hadn't said that. Is it true or did you just want to speak to me?"

"It's true, Polonium poisoning. Recently I got the original autopsy report from a prosecutor. The published one omitted the traces of Polonium found."

Powell was silent. Taking in what I had told him. He would understand the implications.

"The lab boys are sure it was Polonium?"

"One hundred percent, and they identified the specific reactor it came from as the very same one used for the radioactive poison to kill Alexander Valterovich Litvinenko. But there was one very strange thing about Kislitsyn's murder."

"And that was?"

"He was already dying of lung cancer."

"That's what I understood. I kept my eye on things and obtained a copy of the autopsy report when I first heard Kislitsyn had passed away, me being a naturally suspicious gentleman by nature you understand. As you say there was no mention of Polonium in that."

"A coroner called Markov prepared the original report. He had apparently been instructed to remove the Polonium finding from the published report. He didn't say by whom. He left a copy of his original report to be hand delivered to the prosecutor I am working with in the event of his death. Perhaps he was a suspicious gentleman like yourself."

Powell smiled.

"Can I see a copy of this report?"

"I will come to that. I have some other documentation for you to look at."

Although I felt that he was starting to take me seriously and may even believe what I was saying, I also knew he would still suspect anything I gave him directly was a dangle in some attempt to entrap him. My only option was to put all my cards on the table and deal with the consequences, whatever they were.

"Mr. Powell, why would the Russian Intelligence Services want to poison a dying man?"

"Bradley, please. That's a good question. I was hoping you could tell me. Why not just tell me what you know, from the beginning."

"The prosecutor who received the original coroner's report put me in charge of an off books investigation. His name is Litvanov, and he works here in Moscow. He too was a long-term friend of Kislitsyn. I have to admit it was his idea for me to contact you. He was read into Operation RYaN and knew all about the backchannel Kislitsyn and you had running."

Powell gave no indication he was surprised at how much I knew.

"Go on."

"My first assumption was that obviously you would only poison a dying man in order to hasten his death. Second, only a Russian State actor would likely have access to the Polonium that was used to kill him. Third, Kislitsyn was a loyal and reliable officer who didn't get mixed up with office politics and oligarchs. He was not wealthy, didn't mess around with other people's wives and was not a crook. All he did was work. Therefore, I reasoned, Kislitsyn was likely killed because he was working on an investigation someone in the Russian Intelligence Services didn't want him to conclude. That was my working hypothesis. It turns out I was right."

Powell took a moment to take it all in.

"What investigation?"

"It seems Kislitsyn was looking into the ownership and sale of three properties. My recent research revealed the land they were on had originally belonged to the KGB. Checking that information with the land registry apparently set alarm bells off all over the place. Not knowing how big a red flag we had raised we did some more digging and found the houses were linked through an international property agent in Moscow, who confirmed to us they were owned by the same foreign registered company, one registered in Cyprus. Just after that the property agent, a man named Balenkov, was murdered in broad daylight, right before our eyes, on a bridge in the middle of Moscow. I think they knew I was on to him."

"I saw that on TV. A gang related thing they said. Drug deal gone south RT reported. Mind you, it's years since I believed anything they were peddling."

I kept quiet. There was nothing to add to my story.

"So, let me get this straight. You suspect the Russian Intelligence Services of involvement in Kislitsyn and Balenkov's deaths, which you believe are related to the sale of these properties, and your investigation has reached a dead end unless you can get some nice folks overseas to help and you can't ask your bosses, as you suspect they are in on it."

"That's about the size of it. Just as Kislitsyn couldn't trust his bosses during Operation RYaN and came to you for help, now I need to do the same. I need to know who killed my friend."

My plea was drowned out by the clang of the back door. I spun round to see the outline of a man striding toward us.

Powell leaned forward and put his hand on my arm.

"Don't worry, he is with me. You met him at the Embassy yesterday."

As he moved into a shaft of light from the narrow windows by the roof, I recognized him.

"All good Stephen?"

Stephen nodded and settled on the opposite side of the church a few rows in front of us, covering the door we came in. They must have a man outside the back. Powell noticed me checking the exits.

"We have to be careful you understand".

"Yes, I saw your man on the bus."

"Man? He wasn't one of ours. The two old ladies were though."

"Them? They never looked at me once."

"No need, one had a camera in her handbag. I watched you all the way into the bubble from the comfort of my car. I'd hazard a guess you are alone."

I had been taught at Yasenevo that bubble was what people in Powell's world call the surveillance cordon around the target. I guess it went as far as the bus stop where the old lady got off. That must mean a dozen men or so. Impressive, Powell still has more operational pull than he was likely to admit.

"It's just me. The only other I can trust, Kirilov, a new guy who I recruited specifically for this case, is in a safe place with the documents I have for you. Most are originals. I didn't want to bring them tonight, just in case. I have to be careful too you understand."

"This Kirilov, he can get the documents to me?"

"Anytime. I could even have him bring them to the Embassy tomorrow. His is not as familiar a face around here as mine."

"Even so, no need to risk that. Why not have him bring them to the church, say at 11 tomorrow morning. Stephen will be right here to collect them."

"Perhaps I should lend Kirilov my new coat so you can find him?"

Powell smiled. At least he knew I was smart enough to suspect the tracker.

"Yes, I think that would be very wise. Stephen will give Kirilov details of where and when you and I can next meet. I don't want to leave a digital footprint between any of our people and you for nasty little snoopers to find."

Powell got up to head off but turned back when he reached the end of the pew.

"Alexander."

"Yes?"

"Kislitsyn told me all about you years ago. He said if anything ever happened to him, I could trust you. Just you. *Dobroy nochi*, good night."

"*Dobroy nochi*."

Stephen followed Powell out of the church, walking close, but not too close. This guy had training. Whoever he was, he was no embassy desk jockey.

Back outside I ignored the bus and walked to the Metro, sending Kirilov a text to pick me up on foot at the station half an hour or so from the safehouse.

Again, I didn't see him before he caught up with me back at the apartment.

"Did anything catch you eye?"

"No, nothing, all clear."

"Maybe clear of FSB, but I am not sure we could pick out our American friends so easily. They have numbers and they are good. Thank God they are on our side on this one."

I explained to Kirilov the arrangements for him to deliver the documents to the CIA man calling himself Stephen.

"You are to be at the church for eleven. Go the same way I did, the 612 bus. And watch out for little old ladies."

Kirilov was too focused to respond to my joke. He moved the conversation on to what documents we should give to the Americans.

"I think you should take all the originals, but explain to Stephen we need them back for evidential purposes. Well, hopefully, we will need them at some point for evidence."

"And the notebooks?"

"Including the notebooks. I don't know, but maybe Powell's people will be able to verify the handwriting with other documents they have from Kislitsyn. We need to give them all the proof we possibly can. To get help in Cyprus we need them to know we are telling them everything we know. We need them to believe helping us is in their interest too."

"What about one of the thumb drives? They will be able to properly timestamp all the digital documents from the metadata. The timeline will at least back up our story."

"Yes, that can't do any harm. Now let's get dinner and an early night. We have a lot to do tomorrow."

I don't know how easily Kirilov got to sleep, but I was wide-awake. I had far too much going around and around in my head. Foremost in my mind, was what Powell made of it all. I was not sure I was convincing, but Powell letting me know that Kislitsyn had told him he had absolute confidence in me, helped. And he seemed to have the authority to get what he needed. The bubble around our meeting showed that.

He had the pull to get all that sorted in one afternoon. No, it wasn't just my word and the documents. With all the resources at his disposal Powell could conduct his own parallel investigation. I thought about the two old ladies and him watching me on the bus from the comfort of his car. When I eventually fell asleep, I had a peaceful night. It would be my last for some time.

14 WAITING

September 27

I followed Kirilov for an hour, reversing roles and checking for a tail on him. I saw nothing and sent him an all clear text.

When I saw that he was safely on the 612 to meet the Americans I could relax. There was nothing I could do now until he delivered the documents and Powell's people authenticated them. Either they judged the documents legitimate and helped us or they did not. It was out of my control. Needing a drink, I found a café-bar, but stuck to beer to keep a more or less clear head. I could take my time and the beer tasted good.

Into my second I got a text from Kirilov:

'Handover done.'

Not wanting to repeat our mistake with arrangements

for his undercover Balenkov meeting, we agreed for me to pick him up and check his back at Otradnoye Station, keeping to the same routine he had used for me.

Just under an hour of intermittently tense then boring watching and we were back at the apartment. I got there ten minutes before him and grabbed us both a beer. He would need a minute to unwind. I handed him a cold one as soon as he walked in. He swigged most of it in one.

"How did it go?"

"Like clockwork. He doesn't say much, does he? He had a newspaper in a half-open shopping bag ready for me to drop the envelope straight in. He also left me this to use."

Kirilov put a new Korean made cell phone on the table.

"We will get a text with details of your next meeting with Powell, which is set for tonight, no more than thirty minutes before show time. He said keep this phone with you at all times. The meeting will be arranged close enough so you can get there. Once we receive the text, we are to pull the SIM card and throw it and the handset away separately. He will give us a new burner at the meeting. Not taking any chances, are they?"

"No, they are cautious, which is to say professional. From their perspective, until they verify the documents and vet us out, the whole thing could still be some sort of plot to entrap Powell or embarrass the US."

Now they had another way to track my location real time. Who knows, with the phone set up right, even when apparently switched off they could be listening to every word we said. It would be best to assume they were. I wrote that down for him. He didn't seem at all surprised and just nodded. I left the phone where it was, put the tv on and motioned to him to head for the kitchen. Out of habit I leaned over the sink and ran the water as extra cover for our conversation.

"A second meeting arranged for tonight is a quick turnaround. I guess Powell is inclined to believe us, otherwise they would have given themselves more time to plan their next move."

"Could they have checked us out so quick?"

"They can do a lot in a day. They probably have people with access to paid informants in our local police, so they could perhaps have ruled out the official line of a gang hit on Balenkov quickly. As far as we know he didn't have mob connections."

"Cops working for them? I wouldn't have though that likely. Without us knowing anyhow?"

"They will use cutouts. They won't even know who they are ultimately working for. Also, I told them about the prosecutor and Markov. It didn't take Powell long to deduce that nobody except the Russian Intelligence Services has the resources to suppress an autopsy report, assassinate a serving FSB officer using Polonium and then locate and finish off Balenkov within a day of finding out about our inquiry at the land registry? I keep thinking about that and the two men in the van on the bridge. If they had been tailing us then we led the fuckers right to him."

"We had no way of knowing and we had to follow the lead we had. It was all we had."

Nice of him to try, but we both knew I had as much as signed Balenkov's death warrant.

"Anyway, maybe more important than what they have managed to verify is what Powell told me in the church, that years ago Kislitsyn instructed him, that if he was compromised, he could trust me. Only me."

With little to do that afternoon but wait for Powell's message we worked on documenting our first contacts with Powell and progress in the investigation in what would have to pass as a formal report for Litvanov. We made use of Yuri's old Russian made desktop computer, which still used an ethernet cable. Kirilov yanked it out of the wall socket, saying that would put a stop to any SVR or FSB snooping. He joked that he wasn't quite so sure it made it safe from the American cell phone.

The report finished, he wiped the hard drive and packed the few things we had picked up over the last twenty-four hours, ready to move again. I was not sure where to yet. That depended to a large part on what Powell could offer. But one thing was for sure, I had no intention of staying in one place more than one or two nights until this was over.

The new phone buzzed, bang on six o'clock. Another church meeting place and this time in just half an hour. Not enough time for counter surveillance. Taking the street map off Yuri's bookshelf, rather than risk the internet, I found the church was only fifteen minutes away on foot. Looks like they knew pretty much where we were holed up. Now that I was about to meet Powell, the Americans would be checking my back. They had the resources to do a far better job than Kirilov could manage on his own, so I told him he may as well take the evening off.

*   *   *

This time I got to the church before Powell. I didn't notice anyone tailing me, but I knew the Americans had to be. There was no way they would leave Powell wide open in Moscow, even if he was meeting somebody that he said he trusted. They must have figured out I unintentionally led the bad guys straight to Balenkov, so they would conclude there was a risk I could do the same to Powell.

Apart from me the church was empty. I chose a pew near the side exit, a few rows from the back, copying the position they had chosen at the last meeting. Stephen entered the church first, scanning left and right. With only me visible he spoke into his lapel, acknowledging me with a nod, before settling on the last row. A minute or so later Powell entered from a side door. The sweep must be clear. He walked right up and sat next to me.

"*Dobryy vecher*, good evening Alexander, how are you?"

"You tell me."

"You and Kirilov are both clean. We have been keeping a close eye on you, as you will no doubt have guessed. But I do have some interesting news."

"Already?"

"I have friends in high places. The boys back home have identified the numbers which accompanied the three addresses you gave me as IBAN numbers, that is international bank account numbers. They traced two accounts back to the same company based in the UK. The third is for a shell company based in Cyprus, maybe the one Balenkov knew something about. We had some luck checking out the one in the UK. Company records show it is owned by two nominee shareholders."

"And they are?"

"Nobody we are familiar with, yet. It will take a little time, but we will track them down."

"So, you believe me, you can help, you want to help?"

Powell smiled, a disarming spy's smile.

"Of course, I believe you. But quite apart from that, you have given the NSA boys some good leads to overseas companies, shareholders and bank accounts, suspected of links to foreign operations by the Russian Intelligence Services, of which we previously knew nothing. They are, of course, very interested in that. 'Follow the money', as they say in spy school."

"And now what?"

"Now the hardest bit of the game, the waiting. My friend Stephen has left you a new phone on the back row. No need to switch it on until tomorrow but use it at any time in an emergency. Turn it on at ten in the morning every day for an hour. He will contact you when we have something useful with a time and place for us to meet again in person. Likely that will be when we have done a little more digging into the companies and shareholders. It should take no more than a couple of days. Have you got somewhere safe?"

"We will need to move again soon."

"That something we can help you with?"

I hadn't anticipated the Americans would be so accommodating. But this would be a huge weight off my mind. Not only was I running out of ideas for places to go, but I also knew an American safe house would come with American protection.

"At this stage that would be very helpful. It would need to be for both Kirilov and I."

"That won't be a problem. Stephen will send you an address in the morning. That good?"

"Perfect."

"Well then, that's sorted. And I have organized a taxi for you. I can't have you wandering into some bad guys getting back now, can I. Yellow Opel. He will pick you up outside the front entrance in five minutes and take you for a nice little drive before home. Goodnight Alexander."

Powell was on his way before I had time to wish him a good evening. Stephen followed.

Retrieving the phone straight away, I had a few minutes in the silent church to think. Without really planning it that way, Kirilov and I were now all in with Powell and the Americans. I hadn't wanted to get so involved with them, but in the circumstances, how could I turn down their help and protection?

Now the investigation had spread to Cyprus and the UK, we needed their international reach. I suddenly felt the need to swear an oath, to myself as much as the wooden cross before me, that my cooperation with the

Americans would be for this investigation only. For that I had authority from Litvanov. Just like Kislitsyn with his back channel to Powell, I was no traitor.

Outside the church the taxi pulled up just as Powell had said it would. The driver told me Yuri's address before I had chance to say anything. I nodded. He set off in the wrong direction. After crisscrossing the outskirts of Moscow for a half hour he got a one-word message over the radio.

"Clear."

He didn't respond. Neither did I, but inside I was doing cartwheels. It was the first time for days, perhaps since this investigation began, that I could actually be confident the FSB or SVR wasn't following me. Ten minutes later he dropped me right outside the apartment building, zooming off without a word.

Kirilov wasn't around. I made some coffee and settled in to wait, as Powell said, the hardest bit of the game. I must have nodded off in the armchair, waking just before midnight. I went to find Kirilov but he still wasn't back. The peace of mind from hearing the message in the taxi evaporated. I was safe, but what about Kirilov?

15 RESCUE

September 28

An hour later I was frantic. I checked my phone for a message from him for the umpteenth time. There was none. Tired of the waiting, I left a note to text me the instant he got back, then with nothing else to keep me occupied I headed for Tanya's apartment. If he had gone anywhere it would be there and if not there, she might know where he was.

I had no patience for surveillance games. I flagged down a taxi outside the apartment and left the route to the driver. Still I was wary enough to have him drop me a few blocks short of Tanya's. With a chance Kirilov had been picked up it would be wise to check if they had left surveillance on her apartment. For the next fifteen minutes I circled the building on foot, starting wide and narrowing in, but spotted nothing.

Tanya lived in a modern apartment block. I tried the

front door but it needed an electronic fob. Although I was keen to speak to her, despite the hour, I decided to wait for a returning resident before taking the bigger risk of buzzing a ground floor apartment and using my FSB credentials to get in.

The neighborhood was the kind that attracted a late-night crowd, white-collar types in their twenties and thirties enjoying the last blast of freedom before settling down to the suburbs and kids. They had the energy to party and could afford it.

I didn't have to wait long. A taxi pulled up and a couple who looked a little unsteady tottered up to the front door. I made up the distance behind them and a smiling young lady didn't think twice about holding the door for a harmless old man like me. They pressed three on the elevator and continued their loud conversation about how annoying one of their friends had been all night. I pushed the button for the top floor. The lift juddered to a halt. They didn't bother to say goodnight, absorbed in their bitching.

I got out on the top floor, walking round to the back of the building and the freight elevator. I hoped if the apartment was covered at all then it would be just one or two guys at this time of night and that they would be focused on making sure the target stayed home. If they had more people, I was in trouble.

As I descended, I gripped the Makarov in my coat pocket. Its familiar shape was comforting. I had the coat on that Stephen had given me at the Embassy. That gave me some peace of mind too, like I could feel the protection of the Americans.

Unlike the main one, you pulled the freight elevator

door open manually. I cringed as it banged open, my heart in my mouth. I stepped out to see the utility room door was closed. What sounded a cacophony a second ago was probably barely audible in the hallway.

In the gloom I moved along the carpeted corridor as quietly as I could, listening out for any hint of danger. Apart from a muffled TV there was not a sound and allowed my spirits to lift. But approaching the corner my brief optimism vanished with the reflection of a figure in the curved hallway mirror. He seemed to be alone, set up on a chair outside Tanya's door, looking more a guard than part of a surveillance team. He was slumped in his seat, maybe asleep.

It meant he, she or they had been picked up. I backed out the way I came, moving carefully. It was only now, my eyes adjusted to the dim night-lights, that I noticed the small surveillance camera on the wall covering the service elevator. It looked new.

Suddenly I heard a policeman's radio burst into life behind me. I could not make out the broadcast, but as I burst through the service door, I could only figure it was about me.

The FSB may have left a flatfoot outside the apartment but no doubt they would be monitoring the cameras. I punched the button, avoiding the ground floor and potentially bumping into arriving reinforcements, I settled for one up. When the elevator at last got there, I burst into the corridor and battered on the apartment door opposite.

"Police. Open Up. Open Up, Police!"

Someone was still up. A neighboring apartment door opened a few inches and an old man in a dressing gown peeked out. Striding over I thrust my credentials in his face and pushed by him.

"FSB. We have an escapee in the building."

"You people again?"

I made no attempt to reply, making my way through the apartment to the living room, then to the balcony. I could see the front entrance and the street. There was no one yet. The balcony wall wasn't high and there was just a single low railing. I had a chance. Clambering over, I held on for a second before I dropped to the ground. It was further than it looked. My knee buckled as I crumpled in pain.

The old man had put an outside light on and was staring down on me, as neighbors stirred into life, drawing more attention.

"Go back inside. And turn that light out, he has a gun."

It was enough to frighten him.

Now I could hear sirens. Maybe I still had time. Getting to my feet in agony, I began a pathetic limping jog. No more than fifty yards to find cover among unlit trees and bushes.

The Police cars were getting closer. If they knew what they were doing they wouldn't all head straight here, but make a perimeter and close in from all sides. Before I had even caught my breath, sirens sounded from what seemed all points of the compass. This could be it.

My training kicked in. Move and keep moving, turn and keep changing direction. Somehow, despite the pain, I had managed a few blocks as the cars continued to speed by. I stuck to the shadows, resting every time I made cover. I could hear shouted orders, but had no time to listen.

Another car flashed by with lights and sirens on. I crouched in a doorway until it rounded a corner. The adrenalin was running out, my energy draining away and knee pounding. Next second, an unmarked sedan swept out of the darkness. It had no lights on. Cornered in the porch and with my knee killing me there was no chance of escape. They had me.

A mountain in an overcoat emerged from the offside rear door. Neglecting his best Russian an American accent ordered me in. Limping forward I put my hands on my head in anticipation, in my mind already a prisoner. Seeing me struggle the big guy came forward, bundling me in and running around the other side of the car. We accelerated before I had even closed the door, throwing me back in my seat. Still no lights. Looking up I made out Stephen was driving.

"They have Kirilov."

"We gathered."

I heard a siren, close. A marked police car had picked up on us. Stephen put the lights on and accelerated, but they were gaining.

Suddenly I caught a glimpse of a van speeding out of a side street, as I turned it smashed into the side of the police car, T-boning it into a parked car opposite.

"'One of ours."

Stephen stuck to Russian, not the slightest tremor in

his voice.

We slowed at the next corner. Stopping opposite a parked panel van, its rear doors open.

"Let's go."

I didn't need asking twice. Stephen helped me into the back of the van. Pulling the doors shut behind us, he put his fingers to his lips. I could hear another siren approaching. Waiting to be seen, the sedan then shot away, Police car in pursuit.

The vans engine grumbled into life and we headed slowly back in the direction we had come, stopping to let police cars zoom passed us in pursuit of the decoy. Stephen gave me a thumbs-up before he spoke.

"Get some rest. We have a way to go."

There were two mattresses laid out in the back of the van. Wherever we were headed it looked like it was some way from Moscow. Rifling through a first aid kit he produced two tablets, handing them to me with a bottle of water.

"For the pain and the swelling, anti-inflammatory."

I took them gratefully. The adrenaline was gone and my knee was on fire.

"How did you get to me so quickly?"

"The taxi you took was ours. We lost you for a minute after he dropped you off. Who's apartment?"

"It belongs to Kirilov's girlfriend, Tanya. Damn it. I

gave him a night off for fucks sake."

"You can't think of everything. Almost no Ops go to plan. We will find out where he is and get him out."

The American's confidence seemed genuine. I wasn't so sure. Not now. It was even worse in some ways than in Soviet times. People, sometimes important people, journalists and lawyers, who ended up on the wrong side of Putin's clique, got picked up and just didn't make it out. There had been numerous accidents and illnesses, often fatal. I had no doubt that in time Powell's people might find out where he was, but by then it could well be too late.

"Now, seriously, get some rest. We have a long day ahead of us tomorrow."

Exhausted I took the closest mattress and closed my eyes for a minute, expecting nightmares about Kirilov to keep waking me. I was wrong.

When I awoke, I felt groggy and it was broad daylight. Stephen was still sitting in the same place by the van doors. It looked like he hadn't moved.

"*Dobroye utro.*"

"How long have I been asleep? Where are we?"

"You have been out for hours. We are about a hundred miles or so from the Latvian border."

"Latvia, what the fuck are we doing going to Latvia? We need to go back and get Kirilov, now."

"I have been in contact. We haven't located him yet.

And that is not our mission?"

"It's my fucking mission."

I reached for the Makarov that had been in my coat pocket. It wasn't there.

"You looking for this?"

Stephen showed me the pistol. With a practiced hand he removed the magazine, putting the gun in one coat pocket and the magazine in the other.

"What the fuck do you think you are doing... I demand..."

"Take it easy. I have a message from Powell. He says he has his top people working on finding Kirilov and getting him to safety. He feared that you may act, shall we say, rashly."

"So, he exiles me to Latvia?"

"No, he will meet us in Latvia. My job is to get you there. It is a staging post for our trip abroad."

"*Za granitsu*? Abroad?"

"Don't ask me details. I haven't been briefed. Just relax. There's not far to go."

"Where?"

"Nowhere you will know. We are just meeting someone we work with from time to time who will get you across the border. It is safe, there is no need to worry."

His voice was as emotionless as it had been when he rescued me. He may not be worried, but I was sick with anxiety. Feeling like I had abandoned Kirilov to his fate, I sat up straight and leant against the side of the van. My knee was throbbing but I didn't want to risk any more of Stephen's knockout pills.

I tried to calm myself and conserve my energy for my chance to confront Powell. He had no right. No right, but boy did he have the power. I was in no mood for conversation. We sat in silence for the rest of the journey. Stephen seemed more than happy to keep it that way.

16 ESAPE

September 29

The van came to a halt and Stephen opened the rear doors. We were beside a roadside café in a large mainly empty truck park. There were three new dark colored cars parked next to the café, a Mercedes sandwiched between two BMW four-wheel drive crossovers. Powell was already here.

Stephen held the door open for me, but as I went to get out, he put what felt a powerful arm across my chest.

"Just remember who you are talking to in there."

I brushed his arm aside. His boss, no matter how important, was going to get it. He had made me abandon my friend.

I let the café door slam behind me, not waiting for the young American. Seated at a back table facing the door, he was flanked by four formidable looking goons wearing earpieces.

Powell spoke before I could get started.

"Kirilov is dead. I'm so very sorry."

I felt my knees give way. Stephen grabbed me and helped me into a seat. He had anticipated my reaction. He already knew.

Kirilov, dead? He was gone and it was all my fault.

One of Powell's men put a shot in front of me.

"Drink that."

I slugged it back. He poured me another. I went to down that too but Powell put his hand on my arm to stop me. He gripped it firmly, but not in an aggressive way.

"Kirilov was left among the general prison population in Litvanovo. Chechen gang members found out he was a serving FSB officer. They had knives. Mercifully it was quick."

I was numb. He let go of my arm and left me to drink before he continued.

"My friends at Langley have found out what they can about the account numbers you gave us. Two of the bank accounts belong to a holding company registered in Scotland, Highland East Europe Enterprises, but the third belongs to a shell company in Cyprus. Langley has some, admittedly limited, intelligence that Ludmilla Ellena Valentinova, wife of General Valentin, is associated with the Cypriot one."

"*Ublyudok*, bastard, Valentin, I'll kill him."

I went to stand up as if I was going straight back to Moscow to carry out my threat. Stephen and the other man who poured the vodka pushed me back into my seat, not that it took much effort. I had no strength left.

"That is not the way Alexander. We'll get him and whoever is giving the orders, whoever is responsible for Kirilov's death. But we have work to do first, to properly identify all of them. We will get justice for Kirilov, for Kislitsyn, but on our terms. I promise you that."

I looked into his eyes. I don't know if mine told him anything of how I was feeling.

"Langley has given me all they have. To find out more we need to get back in the field, you and me. No time for brooding and any could of, would of, should of, bullshit. And we start now, right now. We are going to find out all about Highland East Europe Enterprises. You are to go by truck with one of our men. He is delivering supplies to the Russian military in the Kaliningrad enclave, but rest assured he works for us and is very reliable. Stephen will fly via Moscow and meet you in Latvia, then bring you to London. I will meet you there."

"London?"

"Highland East Europe Enterprises is a Scottish registered company with the same two nominee directors. They are Lithuanian and Latvian citizens who settled in the UK after studying there. If anyone knows who the real owners of Highland East Europe Enterprises are, it is them. With the help of our friends in London they are going to tell us, one way or another. Then we will find out what this is really all about."

"They'll fucking talk if I get at them."

"They'll talk. I am sure of that. Now I have to go and you need your strength. Order what you want and eat well. It's a long drive for you from here and this could be your last hot meal for a while. The café owner has been taken care of. Our truck driver will pick you up here in about an hour. He will find you."

I stared at him, still lost for words.

"I've been there Alexander. I've lost men in Operations, far too many men. At night I picture their faces, sometimes from years ago. Names, some I have forgotten, but the faces, never. But you have to move, to keep going, to carry on with the mission, to win. You have to. They deserve that and they would do the same for us, if we were the ones on the mortuary slab. You know they would."

Powell stood, put a hand on my shoulder and gripped it tight. His strong grip belied his age. Not a man to be messed with. Then he strode for the exit followed by the goons. He looked a man on a mission. After they had gone, I noticed one of them had left a menu on the table for me. Mechanically I picked it up and ordered. Follow Powell's orders, keep going, one step at a time.

The truck driver arrived before I had finished my food. He gave a flask to the man behind the counter to fill and then came straight over to my table, having no trouble spotting me.

He sat one seat down and one seat over.

"No need for names. I already know what I need to know about who you are. It will be eight hours. I have bread, cheese and coffee. We leave in ten minutes."

He was right, there was no need for names. I didn't want to know his, to get to know anyone else connected to my investigation, even a little. I didn't want to put anyone else at risk. I didn't want to talk. I just wanted to get them, to get even.

Before the ten minutes was up, I was settling down in the truck. I closed my eyes straight away to shut down the chance of small talk. But the driver paid me no attention, knowing better than to bother anybody they wanted moved in this way.

How could I explain all this to Tanya? Her boyfriend, a loyal servant of the Russian Intelligence Services, trapped and murdered by supposed comrades in his own country, albeit at the hands of hired criminal hit men. I was suddenly glad they had not been together all that long. Somebody had to tell her the truth or she would be left to think her boyfriend was a criminal or a traitor, when in reality he had been betrayed by the very worst of those. I promised myself to be the one to tell her, sometime, somehow.

General Valentin. Kislitsyn had hated him from the start, the worst of the new breed of Post-Communist Siloviki, those whose only purpose was to serve Putin and his clan and feather their own nest as they did so. And Valentin had never had any time for Kislitsyn either, or any of the others from what he thought were the KGB old guard. Unsure of their loyalty to the new leadership he had made it his mission to see them off, one by one, sidelining them and pushing them to retirement. Kislitsyn though just wouldn't go. He served the Russian people and the

Russian people alone. More important he retained a few important political allies, connections too powerful to allow an upstart like Valentin to force him out against his will.

Powell was right. I decided I would work with him and his friends as they got what they needed to build a case against Valentin. But when the time came, he was a dead man. Powell may not approve but I knew in my own mind that I wouldn't hesitate for a second to kill him. He was a traitor, a common thief and murderer. I would wait for the opportunity. I would make the opportunity happen if I had to. My thoughts of revenge drifting to wilder and wilder extremes I nodded off to the rhythm of the tires on the road.

The trucks air brakes woke me. We came to a halt in a line of commercial vehicles. Border guards were stopping each one and inspecting papers. My pulse rate rose.

"I'll be on a watch list. I can't show them my papers."

"Don't worry friend. I know them well. We won't be showing any papers."

A fresh-faced guard flagged us to a halt and the driver wound his window down. An older guard with a growling dog, walked off round the back.

"You're out late."

"An urgent delivery for the docks, a part for a missile-cruiser already overdue. The other ships have set off already on another Baltic exercise to annoy the Swedes and they need to catch up."

He shone his flashlight in my face.

"*Kto eto*, who's this?"

I turned away and stared out the side window of the dimly lit cab, not wanting to give him a clean profile, just in case the FSB had circulated my picture this wide. I shouldn't have worried. Powell's man knew his business.

"A right miserable bastard, that's who he is. Those fool EU bureaucrats over the border insist we have a relief driver for trips over six hours, or whatever. It's crazy."

The guard laughed.

"Look you know I'm in a hurry so I'll catch you on the way back to do the paperwork. I have the Navy boys screaming at my boss already. Oh, and tell Dmitri I'll have that German beer for your Saturday night on the return leg."

It was as simple as that. The guard signaled to the gate, the barrier lifted and he waved us on. Without another word, the driver put the truck in gear, released the brakes and seconds later we were on the other side of the border.

I didn't look back.

17 ALIAS

We drove for an hour or so. In the silence I intermittently nodded off, but couldn't settle. The driver looked over and saw I was still awake.

"I will drop you off in about thirty minutes. There is coffee in the flask there."

I helped myself.

As we came up to the half hour there was nothing but darkness and fields. I wasn't being dropped off in a city that was for sure. The last sign named two unpronounceable Latvian towns I had never heard of, three and eight kilometers away. We slowed and he pulled the truck to the side of the road. The truck's headlights caught a parked Skoda.

The driver leaned over to shake my hand. Job done. I shook it, nodding appreciation as I climbed out, slamming the cab door behind me.

Nobody got out to meet me, but I could see the back of someone's head in the driver's seat. The truck set off as I reached the car. Before I got in to see the driver, I heard Stephen's increasingly familiar accent, greeting me in Russian and telling me to put my seatbelt on. As I did, he pulled a U-turn and headed in the opposite direction to the truck, down an empty road.

"There is a travel bag on the back seat. Your wallet is inside. We put an ID together for you. Not perfect, but the best we could do in the time we had. You are a Russian bank official, Anton Markevich. That's what we will tell the Brits, that you are helping us with a foreign corruption case involving a US headquartered multinational energy company. They will buy that, it's not like it would be the first time."

He didn't have to tell me to familiarize myself with the cover story and the documents. The photograph on the Russian passport and identity card had been taken from my FSB credentials, but they had photo-shopped a plain dark suit over my uniform. It was well done and looked like the real thing. With US officials in tow, I had no real concerns the Latvian or British border authorities would look twice.

We hit the main road and headed at speed towards Riga. I guessed we would be flying from the main terminal there but we raced by the airport departures entrance.

"We are going to the Private entrance."

Circling the airport via the main cargo terminal we approached the small chartered flight entrance. The guards must have expected us as they raised the gate before Stephen had slowed below thirty. We drove straight on to the runway apron alongside a small private jet. He jumped out of the driver's seat and before my feet were on the tarmac a man of the same build to the American and wearing a similar dark suit and open collar shirt replaced him. As soon as I had grabbed my bag and slammed the passenger door, the car sped back toward the security gate we just came through, which again rose as the Skoda approached, still accelerating.

"Just a precaution. Your Russian friends have a lot of manpower here."

He gestured up the tiny stairs to the waiting plane. As the engines started to turn, the increasing noise level ruled out conversation. Inside there were ten seats and no other passengers. The door to the cockpit was closed by a uniformed steward with an 'ExecuJet' pin on his jacket lapel. We were already taxiing. Stephen squeezed by me.

"Pick a seat and buckle up. Food and drinks care of Air America."

I couldn't help but smile at his joke, a nod to CIA black ops back in Vietnam days.

"Flight time is only a couple of hours. Thomas Lloyd-Davies our MI6 liaison officer will meet us. You will like him, he is ex-military like us, serving with Special Forces before turning to the dark side."

"I should be careful then."

"Stick to the Russian bank investigator story. We are not going to read the Brits into the Op unless we have to. The less they know the better."

"And tonight, Scotland?"

"Lloyd-Davies says they are driving us straight to a safe house outside Edinburgh. A briefing in the morning from them and partner agencies is scheduled before we make our play at the Latvian and Lithuanian tomorrow. This is a confidential trip, so with a name like Powell coming along there will be no hotels and no commercial travel."

He handed me a buff folder with "Highland East Europe Enterprises" on the front cover. 'Anton Markevich' was printed in Russian in the bottom right corner. Underneath it read 'Senior Investigator – Europe'

They had taken the trouble to make the folder and its contents look used. Background information on the company was in Russian, with copies of documents from UK Companies House and proprietary due-diligence databases printed in English. Scribbled notes in Russian were added in the margins. The handwriting looked like mine, the whole thing a professional job.

Looking up I could see we were airborne. Finding no reason to not take advantage of my Agency provided luxury surroundings I helped myself to a Scotch and Soda before settling in to read up on our targets.

Considering the file more closely, it became clear it was not supposed to contain the whole story. I guessed it was what the Americans had surmised a Russian fraud investigator could have put together, at a distance, about the target companies. It looked like it was designed to convey the impression that we were on to the nominee directors more broadly, but not focused on any other particular companies or accounts. There was absolutely no mention of the specific connections to Russia or Cyprus we had identified.

The Americans were playing their cards close to their

chest on this one, even with their British counterparts. With the private planes, the safe houses and with the cost and risk of bringing me along, it looked like the Agency was taking the investigation seriously. I could see it was important to Powell on a personal level, as Kislitsyn had been a close friend and trusted cooperator, but why would the Agency be so interested? They were throwing resources and money around and seemed content to mislead a close intelligence partner, to some extent at least, about what we were actually up to. There was something more to this than Powell was telling me.

$*$ $*$ $*$

Thomas Lloyd-Davies was just as I had imagined he would be. Over the years I had read reports from our Spetsnaz forces who had come into contact with British SAS troop in Afghanistan, Iraq, Syria and elsewhere. Unlike the Spetsnaz, the SAS men tended to be smaller, leaner and quieter. But like them they were, by all accounts, very tough and very capable.

Davies was about five nine and looked the agile type, not too muscular. I guessed he was no more than one hundred and fifty pounds. He walked forward to meet us as I descended the staircase from the executive jet.

"Stephen, good to see you again, and this must be Anton. Delighted."

He held out his hand. A limp, lukewarm, handshake, I immediately thought offered that way to disguise his strength and background. He may be ex-special forces but he clearly now enjoyed the ready deception skills of the spy and spy catcher world.

"Gentleman, I'm sorry to say there's no time to hang about. We've got a couple of comfortable cars ready and it's straight off I'm afraid. Should make Edinburgh in about four hours, tops."

He led us to the two Range Rovers and we split up. Stephen joined Davies in the lead car while I was guided to the back of the second vehicle with two serious looking types occupying the front seats. Sandwiches and a flask of coffee had been left for me on the otherwise empty back seat. They never spoke and I was glad for the silence. Putting on your cover can be exhausting and the more you said, the more chance you would fuck it up.

I noticed a big blue highway sign that said 'M25'. That was the last thing I remember before one of the men in the front seat welcomed me loudly to Scotland.

"That's the border. It's forty minutes from here."

Still half asleep I watched the lampposts flash by as we continued to ignore the speed limit. The tempo was broken as we exited onto a single carriage road and slowed down as the forest enveloped us. We soon seemed a world away from highways and airports.

Without warning we swung off the road between two stone stags and onto a gravel single-track path. It took a couple of minutes to reach the dark gothic house the gateway belonged to. It was worth the wait. As the trees separated, they revealed a steel grey lake, with a vista of hills and snow-capped mountains as a backdrop.

"Welcome to Lakeside, Sir."

The other silent front seat passenger leapt to his feet

from the still rolling car before I had time to reach for my seatbelt.

Lloyd-Davies walked towards me from the house, his driver having won the race to our destination. Stephen was nowhere to be seen.

"Anton, bit of a change of plan, Mr. Powell has nipped off for a bit of dawn fishing with my boss Phil tomorrow morning, so they will catch up with us later at the briefing. Your room is ready. The butler will show you the way. They have left some dinner for you, so make yourself at home and try and get a good night's kip, you must be tired after your long journey."

If only he knew how long a journey. After me extraction Moscow seemed a world away.

'Kip', another damned word I didn't recognize. In the context it must mean sleep, but I couldn't recall. I remembered my KGB English teacher prior to my posting had taught me to forget any notion of the 'Queens English' when you got there. He instructed us to be prepared for a 'cacophony of colloquialisms' on arrival. You could tell he liked the sound of those words rolling off his tongue, he used them often to help us with our pronunciation. I never got it right, as he didn't tire of telling me.

My room looked like a set from those old Sherlock Holmes 'B movies' I had gotten to like so much in London all those years ago. Bare sandstone walls with tapestries, paintings, swords and shields. A creaky polished wooden floor and ancient noisy plumbing added to the effect.

The butler, who must have been in his late seventies if he was a day, showed me to my room, hovering for a tip I couldn't provide as Stephen had neglected to give me any money. I guess he thought I wouldn't get far without any cash if I decided to run for it.

Even after the sandwiches in the car I made light work of the steaming hot beef stew that had been left for me. Fed, warm and comfortable I checked the landing through the spy-hole. There was a man with a big overcoat and an earpiece standing outside my bedroom door. I was not sure if he was there to keep me in or the bad guys out, or maybe even a little of both.

18 SCHEME

September 30

The meeting room at Lakeside was large and modern, out of character with rest of the house. The table was a period piece that could seat twenty or more. Traditional family portraits and swords from battles against the English adorned the walls, contrasting with the state-of-the-art comms and videoconference screens that had been set up.

By the time Stephen led me to my seat next to Powell almost all the seats at the table were occupied. The initially hushed tones got louder as small huddles of conversation broke out. I couldn't figure out why there were so many people at the meeting. This was supposed to be a secret mission for God's sake. Powell walked over.

"What are all these people doing here?"

"Alexander, you might well ask. There have been some

developments while you've been asleep. The shit has hit the proverbial fan in both Washington and Langley. We had better get started."

Washington? And Powell had just addressed me as Alexander, abandoning my cover without explanation.

"Good morning ladies and gentlemen, please take your seats, we've a lot to get through. First, let me introduce you to Alexander, a serving Major of the FSB, who came to us with a very interesting story about the murder of his boss."

I was stunned. My name, rank and the core of our investigation revealed to a room of complete strangers. I half expected Powell might want me to address the meeting, but before I had time to panic, he began explaining the case himself, from the beginning.

The lights lowered and Stephen, using a wireless tablet, produced a grainy picture of Kislitsyn on the screens with 'MI5' prominently displayed in the top left corner. No doubt the logo was a sign of who was in charge for colleagues in what Security Service officers typically regarded as inferior services and agencies.

Powell told the story well, a natural performer used to big stages. As Powell got to our arrival in the UK to follow up on the nominee directors, the lights went up. Lloyd-Davies had slid quietly into one of the seats at the table opposite Powell.

The young Englishman took over the meeting.

"So, there you have it ladies and gentleman, the picture as of yesterday evening. However, it seems Langley doesn't sleep and by the time we awoke we had an update from the Cousins that has put the cat among the proverbial pigeons. Bradley perhaps you could fill everyone in?"

"My folks back at Langley, with the help of the NSA, have been doing a bit of digging around the account numbers and companies Alexander tipped us off about. The bottom line is, it turns out Highland East Europe Enterprises is linked to a company called UKRAINImport. Now, UKRAINImport is a Latvian based shell company which our sources locally say is a vehicle to move money to pay Ukrainian rebels and militias. These militias are being used by the Russians as proxies in Crimea and are the ones who have occupied eastern Ukraine on their behalf. In a nutshell, we think the whole scheme was set up by elements in the Russian Intelligence Services to covertly provide foreign hard currency to finance their proxy forces. It looks like Kislitsyn may have gotten too close to figuring this out for the Kremlin's liking. So, our little murder investigation is now a major sanctions issue of significant interest to the White House. As Langley has been all too keen to make crystal clear to me."

An unremarkable middle-aged woman in a tweedy suit that looked too old for her interrupted Powell with a question.

"Sarah Langdon, Treasury Task Force. When you say 'think' Bradley, exactly how sure are you?"

"Ma'am, my apologies, I should have been clear. When I said we think, I meant we assess, and with some confidence. The NSA came up with some financials and my side of the house corroborated their findings with some friendly folks in the banking game. We are pretty sure our Latvian sources are correct, but now this is a sanctions issue, we need to prove it."

"John Cleverley, HMRC Liaison. Just to reinforce what Bradley said we have observed transfers for the same entities and concur with Langley's assessment. This does look like a Russian scheme to covertly finance undesirables in Crimea and Ukraine."

Lloyd-Davies continued as chairman, nodding to his colleagues in turn as he spoke.

"Thank you, John, Sarah. So, there we have it. The significance of the assessment from our American friends meant I wanted all interested parties to get their heads together and see how we can assist. Can you tell us what it is you need from us Bradley?"

"OK. So, now we have direct interest from the White House itself. As you know, the new President's attempted olive branch to Putin has gone south. Meaning, he now wants to show he is being tough with Russia, who just aren't playing nice. He is all over the Treasury and State Department to pile more sanctions on Russian individuals and entities connected to the Kremlin, particularly those meddling in Ukraine. And to do so as soon as possible. Our little investigation has been identified as an ideal opportunity for us to do just that."

"And what can we do, specifically?"

"We need solid evidence to get the Treasury and State Department people on board. Let's just say that in the past they have acted on what the Agency said was rock solid intelligence and been burned. I want to build, step by step, on Alexander's investigation and give them documented proof. The Treasury and State Department folks want all the I's dotted and T's crossed before they act. So, let's pay a visit to the registered Lithuanian and Latvian directors of

Highland East Europe Enterprises and put the squeeze on. We need to conclusively identify the people behind that company for a start. Can you guys help us with that?"

Cleverley from HMRC jumped in first, ahead of an older looking man on my left who hadn't spoken, but was obviously keen to say something.

"Well, strictly speaking nominee directors have the same responsibilities as ordinary directors. It is an offense to deliberately obscure beneficial ownership, or assist in setting up and running shell companies for that purpose."

The other man his chance and spoke up. A brusque Scot with a strong accent, overweight, scruffy and with an unkempt, graying red beard.

"Balls. You haven't managed a meaningful prosecution for one of those for years, if bloody ever, and it could take months."

"Could you identify yourself to the meeting please?"

"Why not, McArthur, UK Border Force or whatever they call us this week. That's immigration to you Yanks and Russians. No, the way to put the heat on these bastards is to wave their immigration status and leave to remain in their faces. False statements from both when they arrived on student visas in 2003. Handily, that was before Lithuania or Latvia joined the much-lamented European Union that we all can't wait to leave."

If anyone thought this was a good idea, they kept it to themselves. Not in the least phased by the lack of verbal support McArthur carried on.

"Don't you see? They haven't taken the trouble to

notify immigration of any changes to their home address, or employment or marital status since. So, technically speaking, their status needs to be clarified, before we could possibly say, categorically, they actually have leave to remain. Of course, while we conclusively establish their legal status, we have the power to detain them, if we, say, conclude they pose a flight risk. And for our purposes, I would suggest, we, most definitely, do so conclude."

The room fell silent again. I liked him but sensed he wasn't popular with his more polished colleagues from other agencies. For me he was just the man I would want to put pressure on the nominee directors. Powell jumped in.

"Interesting, that seems a darn good place to start to put the squeeze on the targets to me. Tom, do you agree?"

"Absolutely. In no way subtle, but it could get the job done."

McArthur had no interest in making friends.

"Subtle, bollocks."

McArthur was again met with momentary, uncomfortable, silence.

"Perfect. That fits the bill from the US end and as no one seems to object, Alexander, what are you thinking?"

I looked up from my doodling of the coat of arms on the crested notepad in front of me.

"*Khorosho*, fine. It works for me."

"Excellent, that would seem to be the way forward

then."

"Just one more thing Mr. Powell."

"What's that Alexander?"

"Mr. McArthur here, he does the pitch."

*   *   *

Less than two hours later we were on the highway. We had come out of a very beautiful forest and were speeding towards our targets in a suburb of Edinburgh.

McArthur sat next to me, with Powell in the front. Lloyd-Davies followed with the HMRC man Cleverley. I felt a gentle elbow in my ribs and turned to find McArthur offering me a hip-flask he had produced from somewhere in his dirty raincoat.

"Best Scotland has to offer."

I took a swig. The whisky was peaty and smooth, as good as I'd tasted. Head and shoulders above the counterfeit hooch labeled as Scotch in the bars I frequented in Moscow.

"That's good Scotch. What brand is it?"

"Single malt, from the Isle of Islay, my birthplace."

It was the first thing McArthur had said since we left Lakeside and I was glad of the opportunity to break the ice. I motioned to him to offer some to Powell, but McArthur shook his head and had the flask back in his coat pocket in an instant.

"Where is Islay?"

"It's off the West coast. It's a beautiful island, so it is. I grew up there. My father was a farmer, in his later years."

"And before?"

"Navy."

"My Father was military too, a Guard."

"And you followed him into the forces by the look of you."

"I was with the Army, signals, before Kislitsyn took me with him to the KGB."

"Signals. Clever boy. I was just a grunt."

McArthur had that bearing and look that men have when they have seen bloody war. Something in the eyes and a separateness from those who have not served. I had seen it in many men in Russia I had worked with over the years.

"Abroad?"

"Falklands, 1982. Goose Green."

He said Goose Green as if I should recognize it. I did my best to conceal that I had never heard of this battle. The Falklands I knew about. The KGB had assessed that with their shrinking Navy there was no way the British could support land forces on the distant islands. Like the Argentineans they had been completely mistaken.

"You?"

"Not so much abroad. Counter-Intelligence, at home mainly."

We fell back into silence and I wondered what images this old British soldier was conjuring up of my Counter-Intelligence work for the Sword and the Shield. They may not have been good.

"What was he like, your Colonel Kislitsyn?"

I thought for a moment.

"You."

"Me? What do you mean?"

"He didn't suffer fools gladly and he had no reservations about telling his lazy or incompetent superiors exactly what he thought of them."

McArthur burst out laughing. The kind of raucous belly laugh I thought was reserved for the stage. Powell, who must have been dozing, turned around and asked what was funny.

"Nothing. Just my Russki friend here telling me what a fine upstanding gentleman Kislitsyn was."

Not privy to our joke, Powell returned to his snoozing.

McArthur produced the hip-flask again.

"Old Comrades."

"*Tovarishchi*, comrades."

We toasted our fallen friends and fellow survivors, both lost in private thoughts of bungled operations, bloody firefights and the occasional acts of genuine heroism we had witnessed.

19 JULIJA

As we approached the ring road the Edinburgh sky darkened. When the rain came, it seemed to be coming in horizontally. It was amazing how often and how quickly the weather turned here.

We left the highway and were soon among street after street of pretty two and three-story stone row houses. A few turns later, the traditional stone buildings were mixed with modern, less attractive, brick buildings. They looked out of place. Mitchell Street was divided with new three-story apartment blocks on one side and period Victorian walkups on the other.

Our two Land Rovers pulled up behind a parked van with signage advertising 'Electrical Services You Can Afford'.

McArthur took command. It was his patch after all.

"Welcome to Leith. Wait here."

He got out of the car and struggled into his dirty raincoat before walking up to the van. The driver's window wound down despite the driving rain. Any conversation was short.

He returned and held the door open.

"She's in. Let's go."

A circular hand signal from McArthur was enough to empty the van and the other Land Rover. The group huddled round McArthur for instructions as Powell and I held back.

"You two back, you two front, Mr. Powell, Alexander, Jimmy with me".

The uniformed Border Force officers made off to their allotted posts as we followed McArthur. Approaching the entrance, the workman tinkering with the circuit breakers in the hallway, opened the door.

"2F, second floor."

McArthur led us up the stairs. To one side of the apartment door, he raised a palmed hand signaling us to stop and beckoned Jimmy forward. Now I noticed Jimmy's stab-proof vest read 'POLICE' rather than 'Border Force' like the others.

McArthur motioned for Powell and I to stay put and put his finger on his lips. We remained silent. Out of habit, I reached for my righthand coat pocket where I usually kept the Makarov when on a raid. I felt naked without it.

Jimmy knocked the door.

"Hello. Police Scotland. Is anyone in?"

He waited a second or two then banged the middle of the door hard with the side of his fist. It rattled on its hinges.

"Police Scotland. Open up."

Inside, footsteps on an uncarpeted floor. The door opened.

"Good morning madame, Police Scotland, may we come in? I have a few questions for you."

Without waiting for a reply Jimmy eased himself by whoever was there.

"Thank you. Is it just you at home today madame?"

"Yes, yes, it is. What's this about?"

McArthur strode forward.

"Good morning, Miss Julija Grinevskis is it?"

Powell and I followed McArthur into the apartment. By now Jimmy and McArthur had made it across the hallway and into the open-plan living room.

"It is, and who exactly are you?"

She sounded indignant, whereas McArthur was a picture of calm.

"McArthur, UK Border Force, I have some questions about your immigration status."

She didn't respond immediately and was clearly rattled when she did.

"Immigration status? I am Scottish and I have been here for years. What the hell are you talking about?"

"Well, that could be true if you had entered Scotland legally, but, I'm afraid, that doesn't seem to be the case."

"What? I'm European, Lithuanian by birth. It's in the fucking European Union in case you didn't know!"

McArthur didn't raise his voice.

"Yes, quite right, but that's rather the point. You see it wasn't in the European Union when you arrived in 2003 and in relation to another matter altogether, I've been looking into the history of your case. Jimmy, could you pop out and get me my case files. Sorry, in the rush I seem to have left them in the car. Back seat I think."

Jimmy departed with a nod.

At the mention of 'the 'case files' and 'rush' Julija's face had turned from anger to something else entirely. She slumped down on the sofa.

"Case, what case? I don't understand."

"Well, it might just be a mistake and nothing to worry about, but then again."

She stood up, defiant rather than angry.

"I have had enough of this. I am calling my solicitor."

"I wouldn't do that, just yet. There may be no need to

go to all that trouble. And there will be plenty of time for the legal stuff at the immigration hearing".

"Immigration hearing? I live here! I have for years, I am Scottish and I pay my taxes like anyone else, for Christ's sake."

"As you said. It's just that your visa application was for a student named Julija Grinevskis from Vilnius, is that you?"

"Yes, of course it's fucking me. Who else would it be?"

"Good, good. Then, perhaps you could show me some proof of your status as a student at the time and we can clear up this misunderstanding and that will be the end of it. A copy of your Diploma or graduation certificate perhaps?"

She sat down on the sofa again.

"I haven't, I mean I didn't get to actually graduate. I had met Kaspars by then, and there was just no need."

"Ah, yes, that would be Mr. Kaspars Vējonis. It's in the file, but you see, he seems to have the same problem as you. He arrived on a dubious student visa too. We will be seeing him later today."

The apparent seriousness of the situation seemed to be dawning on her and perhaps memories of a real fear of people 'in authority' dating from her youth. Vilnius under the Communists was a far cry from here.

"That's the ticket. Let's just all calm down and have a nice sit down and figure this out. Perhaps we could have some tea while Jimmy gets the paperwork, then we can get that done and hopefully be on our way and leave you in peace."

"Tea. Yes, of course. The British cure for everything."

Julija headed to the kitchen, defeated.

Powell beat me to it.

"Nice work McArthur. Have you perhaps, done this kind of thing before?"

McArthur grinned.

"Just the once or twice laddie, look and learn. And drink your bloody tea, no matter if its gnat's piss. And that goes for you as well Russki."

Powell flashed me a smile.

Jimmy returned with an old leather briefcase and handed it over. McArthur took out a slim buff folder with 'Julija Grinevskis' written by hand in neat marker pen on the front cover. It only had a few pages in it. Quickly McArthur pulled a stack of papers from two other folders and stuffed them at the back of the Grinevskis file. An old pro, who knew the oldest tricks in the book.

She returned with a tray. Teapot, cups, milk jug and sugar bowl, all matching. She put it down on the coffee table and disappeared back to the kitchen without a word, returning with a plate of chocolate cookies. She couldn't keep her eyes off the file McArthur had left at the other end of the coffee table, as he occupied himself lumping three heaped spoons of sugar in his tea. He took his time and tapped his teaspoon loudly three or four times on the side of the cup, when he was eventually done stirring.

"Now Julija, I should really go through this entire file and check what's what with you in detail, but if you can help us out with one or two things then maybe we can get through it all in a jiffy. Perhaps we won't have to bother Mr. Vējonis at all. Shall we see how we go?"

Julija nodded, seeming very keen on not bothering Mr. Vējonis, another good call from the wily Scottish officer.

"So, we established you didn't finish your studies, so what did you do to support yourself back then Julija?"

"I worked part time at a café, that's where I met Kaspars."

"I see, I see."

McArthur picked up his thick 'Julija Grinevskis' file and started making notes. Julija looked concerned. McArthur sat well back on the low sofa, meaning she had no chance to see what he was writing.

Again, he took what seemed an age finishing what he was, or wasn't, actually writing, stoking the tension.

"So, you were working before you met Mr. Vējonis. But you didn't have a work visa, that right?"

"Yes, I mean no. I didn't, but it was only a few hours a week."

"I see. And after you met Kaspars Vējonis and left your studies you worked a few more hours, did you?"

"Yes, I suppose I did more hours."

Another note, written excruciatingly slowly.

"How many more hours?"

"Look, it was a long time ago, I can't be sure".

"Well, it could be important you see, to the outcome. I just want to establish the facts."

McArthur took a slurp of tea.

"Oh, I don't know twenty hours a week or so, maybe a few more, I guess. Only for a while though, before I had Maria."

"Maria, yes your daughter. How old is she now?"

"Twelve."

McArthur added to his file.

"A lovely age, twelve. And she's at school at the moment, correct?"

"Yes."

"Well, no need to worry on that account, she was born here so she's fine."

The clear implication that she was fine but her parents may not be was not lost on Julija, or anyone else.

"Now, have you got someone to look after Maria while we straighten things out?"

"Look after her, what do you mean?"

"Well, we may have to detain you temporarily, and Kaspars too, just until we can get hold of a Magistrate and maybe argue you are not a flight risk and don't need to be kept in detention, due to the peculiar circumstances of the case that is, pending the hearing of course.'

"No, no, that's not possible. It's just Kaspars and I. You can't, she's just a wee girl."

She was reaching breaking point. McArthur knew it.

"Well, to be fair to the child, perhaps if you could help us out with something, I could put in a word for you that you were currently actively assisting with a priority investigation, of great value to the Crown, and needed to remain at liberty to continue to do so. Do you think you could you possibly do that?"

She looked resigned.

"What? What is it you people want?"

"Information, that's all, just a tiny bit of information we know you have ready access to. These two nice quiet gentlemen here have traveled a very long way. They need to know who the beneficial owners of Highland East Europe Enterprises are, and they need to know now. If you can give us that information now, we will walk out of here and I promise you will never hear from any of us or the Border Agency again. On my life."

She wavered. Instinctively McArthur seemed to know why.

"And there's no reason Kaspars has to know about our little visit, no reason at all."

With that, she left the room. McArthur winked at me as Powell gave him a thumbs up.

Julija came back with a bright blue ring binder. It was the cheap kind you could buy at any supermarket. Taped on the front was a neat printed plastic label: 'Highland East Europe Enterprises'.

Julija handed it to McArthur.

"You can't take it with you, he will notice."

"No need. My friends here just need a quick peek and then we will all be on our way."

He passed the file to Powell, who couldn't help himself, opening it up on the coffee table. Julija for some reason seemed to need to look away, as if she didn't want to witness a crime.

McArthur took the cue and started clearing the tea cups before leading her back to the kitchen, offering to help clean up. Powell leafed through the thin file. I couldn't wait either, leaning over for a glimpse.

The first pages were the incorporation documents naming Julija Grinevskis and Kaspars Vējonis as Directors of Highland East Europe Enterprises, which we had already seen. Powell turned to the last page and there it was.

A simple photocopy of a single check for a mere seven hundred pounds sterling, payable to Kaspars Vējonis. It was a company check from 'UKRAINImport Ltd.' No doubt payment to set up Highland East Europe Enterprises.

The check was dated January 2009. By my reckoning, then, the Russian Intelligence Services had kept the company on the shelf ready to use for more than five years. Good to know, but of far more importance the check was drawn on a UKRAINImport Ltd account with 'eBank of Cyprus' and signed by someone named Karius Kargin.

We had just what we had come for. A name, a signature, and even better, a bank and a bank account number. Powell took his phone from his pocket to photograph the check. I could see the screen as he sent the text. The recipient was a US number starting '+01', with no name visible. Presumably someone at Langley or the NSA. Powell closed the file and put it back on the coffee table.

"Let's go."

Making the hallway, McArthur and Jimmy were chatting quietly to Julija. Seeing us McArthur took a photograph out of his pocket. It was a mug shot of a dark-skinned teenager, possibly Arabic. He showed the photo to Julija. The friendly tone he had adopted towards the end of their conversation was gone.

"If anyone asks, this is the absconder from the immigration detention center we were here looking for. Say we said he had been seen locally. His name is Ahmed Attaf. Obviously, you have never seen him before. It would be best for you if you stick to that story and never mention our interest in Highland East Europe Enterprises, to anyone, not even Kaspars."

He handed the photo to Jimmy.

"Now Jimmy, take one of the uniform boys and do a house to house for Mr. Attaf. Use the same story. Check with every apartment on this street."

McArthur didn't miss a thing. He led us out of the apartment with a smile and a simple "thanks" in the direction of a visibly deflated Julija.

20 CYPRUS

In the car on our way back from Edinburgh Powell had been occupied on his laptop. When we pulled into the drive back at Lakeside, he told me that I would be flying out with him in a couple of hours to Cyprus to follow up on the bank lead. All the way back, I had been working out a way to ask him if I could do just that.

Walking into the house, I found myself with Powell, a little behind the others.

"Alexander, come with me for a minute, we have time before we need to leave for the airport."

I followed Powell down a narrow dark stone hallway to a door opposite the conference room we had met in. Powell opened it without knocking.

An Agency man I had seen but not been introduced to was standing by an open laptop on an otherwise empty desk in the smaller sparsely furnished meeting room.

"Is it ready?"

"Yes Sir."

"O.K. Get it running and then scoot."

The unidentified CIA agent pressed a few keys and then headed out, closing the door behind him. Powell locked it.

"Take a seat."

He swiveled a chair round for me, pressed a combination of keys, then stood aside.

A video started running and as the screen brightened, I recognized the man who was bound and gagged to a kitchen chair. Two burly men wearing dark coats and balaclavas stood either side of him.

A voice speaking unaccented Russian came from a third person off camera.

Powell leaned over and paused the video.

"Do you know him?"

I nodded.

"We know all about him. He is from the good old days in Department V of the First Chief Directorate, Ivanov, right?"

"Yes, that is him. But what you may not know is what a sadistic bastard he is, but when did you...?"

Powell cut me off.

"We grabbed him yesterday returning home, drunk. He lives on his own, I understand."

"He has an unorthodox lifestyle."

"We gathered. Who in their right mind would live with a sociopath like him? Just watch."

This time I pressed the 'play' key.

"Ivanov, wake up, look at me."

One of his minders shook him awake.

"Ivanov, this needle I am holding contains a new experimental and powerful drug we are using to help people with, shall we say, recalling events they may not want to."

Ivanov's eyes widened.

"It is very effective, very. The only problem is that it appears to be unreliable, in terms of after effects. Some of the tests left people with lasting memory loss and, other more troublesome emotional problems."

His eyes widened further. He began shaking his head.

"But if you provide honest answers, immediately, to the three simple questions I have, then I would have no need to use the drug and we will be on our way. Answer without hesitation. You will get only one chance, one. Be aware we already know a lot about this matter. This will be obvious from my questions. Do you understand?"

Ivanov nodded.

"Do not make any noise other than the answers to my questions. Not a sound. Got it?"

He nodded again.

"Remove the gag."

The gorilla on the right untied the knot behind his head and pulled it away. The prisoner wretched and coughed before he caught his breath.

"Right, we begin. Did General Valentin order Colonel Kislitsyn's death?"

He mumbled a barely audible reply.

"Louder please, for the camera."

"*Da.*"

"Was Polonium poising used to kill Kislitsyn?"

"*Da.*"

"Did you carry out Valentin's order to poison Kislitsyn?"

Ivanov hesitated, weighing up the consequences of his answer. The needle appeared back in camera shot.

"You will answer immediately, or else so help me."

His eyes changed, he was enraged, defiant. He screamed the answer.

"*Da! Da!*"

The two men in camera grabbed him and the one who had removed the gag forced it back in his mouth, again tying it behind his head. The other one raised his sleeve. Ivanov struggled and tried to kick out but these men knew their business well and easily overpowered him.

A man from behind the camera appeared carrying a needle. He too had a balaclava. From his voice I could tell he had been the one asking the questions.

"Don't worry, this is just a sedative so we can make a leisurely exit. That stuff about psychotic drugs was all bullshit."

If anything, Ivanov's eyes showed greater fury as the two men held him down and the interrogator thrust the needle into his arm.

Powell closed the laptop.

"Ivanov, that fucking psychopath, I should have guessed."

"A convincing confession though don't you think? Something we can make good use of should there be any doubts or denials later on."

"Who were the Russians in balaclavas?"

"They would say they are Ukrainians. We picked them up in Donbass early after the Russian invasion. They were making plenty of trouble for the little green men in unmarked uniforms from over the border. Now they are contractors we use from time to time. They are very good, very discreet."

"Contractors?"

"Welcome to the modern world Alexander. Deniability and economics are the name of the game my friend. And we don't have to worry about funding pensions for these guys."

*   *   *

We landed at Larnaca that night. Once again Stephen had gone ahead. I was told this time flown out by the US Air Force from RAF Lakenheath. He was there to meet Powell and I as we descended the few steps off the private aircraft. Two large vans with blacked out windows were waiting, with their attentive drivers, both wearing earpieces, standing by.

A warm Mediterranean breeze greeted us. It was welcome after the constant drizzle of my first few days back in the UK for what seemed an eternity.

Stephen was all business, but he was smart enough to know seniors like us two would not be fit for much after the day we had and the late flight, so he kept it brief. He didn't introduce me to the other Agency men, but did tell me we were checked in at a small boutique hotel in Limassol. He described it as not too flashy, but big enough for the surveillance teams and only five minutes from the center of town. Teams? These guys weren't messing around. I don't know where Powell got his energy, but he had questions.

"What's the set up?"

"We have two surveillance teams in the hotel and a

fallback safehouse picked out should the hotel be compromised. You, Alexander and I have three rooms on the same floor. One team is rotating on the bank and the other on Valentin's wife, Ludmilla Ellena Valentinova. We had only been on the bank for a matter of hours when Valentinova showed up."

"And tonight?"

"Nothing. You two need a good night's sleep. I will get the team leaders' reports tonight and brief you over breakfast, say zero eight hundred."

Powell seemed satisfied. And Stephen was right that I, for one, was exhausted. I had been on the go for days. He put us in the second van. I had already closed my eyes before we left the airport perimeter. My nap was short. It was only a fifteen-minute drive to our hotel north of the city.

*   *   *

October 1

I had arranged to meet Powell for breakfast and I was just fifteen minutes or so late, which by my early in the day standards wasn't bad. I was apparently not a 'morning person', as Viktoriya never tired of reminding me.

Powell had picked a table by the open rear windows through which a pleasant breeze was blowing. As the ranking spy, he got the seat facing the breakfast room, the likeliest direction of any trouble. He had also strategically placed himself on the side nearest the exit.

"Cyprus has changed a lot since you were last here

Alexander."

He couldn't hide his smile, knowing I would not be able to resist checking out his source.

"Oh, and when was that?"

"It was August, 1976. You and Kislitsyn were sent to pick up a delivery boy who was supposed to be making a cash drop to Black September but had gone rogue and started splashing cash all over Limassol like it was Christmas and he was the sainted *Ded Moroz* himself."

It was my turn to smile. I couldn't remember the couriers name but I remembered the story and the year was about right. The courier had lost it when he found out his wife was having an affair with a KGB Colonel back home. The adulterer was a desk jockey from the Center who had never worked abroad, unlike the courier who had been running around the Middle East for months, bankrolling Arafat and whoever else could shoot up an El Al departure lounge. He must have been well connected though, as from what I recall, when we eventually dragged him home, he was demoted and given a desk job. It could have been much worse, with others in those days paying the ultimate penalty for such indiscretion.

"Cyprus has changed how?"

"Well, there are so many of your countrymen washing their money here now, that there are Russian supermarkets on the high streets, all selling your favorites from back home and happy to display the prices in Cyrillic. Would you believe there are now more Russian banks on this tiny little island than there are in the whole of Germany. Any of your compatriots who need a less conspicuous passport is in luck. If they invest five hundred thousand Euros or more in a Cypriot business, EU citizenship courtesy of the Government of Cyprus is theirs in six months, with seemingly no questions asked."

I liked Powell, he made me laugh.

"Vodka, borscht and pickles it is then, my treat."

"Not a chance, I am going to find a waiter to get us a real breakfast. They must do waffles, though I think I will be pushing it to ask for my grits and biscuits."

From the open hotel balcony, I could see down the narrow street. Cyprus may have modernized in the ways Powell described but to me the beautiful stone architecture which abounded, remained timeless.

Stephen appeared from my blindside. He had a way of stealthily showing up that was disconcerting to say the least.

"Good morning, Alexander, where's the boss?"

"He is tracking down a waiter, should be back shortly. Coffee?"

Powell returned with a very pretty, tanned, shy young lady in an immaculate white blouse, dark blue waistcoat and bow tie in tow. She seemed keen to take our orders as quickly as she could and escape the brash foreigners. I had heard the locals described as quiet, even a bit dull, but I think unassuming was more accurate. Ordering nothing, Stephen was as keen to get on with the briefing as waitress had been to leave.

"I have the team leaders' reports."

Powell picked up his cup.

"Go on."

"Team one is on the eBank Cyprus branch Ludmilla Ellena Valentinova and UKRAINImport use. We have confirmation from Langley that they receive regular wires of large sums to UKRAINImport there. No current trace for Karius Kargin, the guy who signed the check. Looks like he's left the company or that particular alias has been retired."

"Perfect. We have the accounts and the money coming in, now we need to trace where it goes when Valentinova picks it up."

"Valentinova is living the high life here. House by the sea, servants, personal trainer, yacht club, nice car, designer shops, the lot. The boys and I have been speculating and are generally agreed on a hypothesis that Valentin would only have his wife handling the money personally if he was taking a cut for himself. Otherwise he would have some poor schmuck from Moscow Center holed up in a two-bit guesthouse couriering the cash on the cheap. Now if that were true and we can catch him and the lovely Mrs. V pocketing cash, then we can put the screws on him and who knows, maybe even get a cooperative witness. Now that should shut the bean counters at Treasury up."

Powell put down his coffee.

"And in light of this hypothesizing, your plan would be?"

"Our immediate objective should be to track down Valentinova's bank accounts. To this end Alpha team leader, Brad, has hired a local lawyer to approach the Bank for a loan for a shelf company we have up and running. It's a sizable deal for the branch and negotiations will helpfully be protracted. The manager has arranged for us to have use of a small conference room at the bank. We have checked it out and from there we have eyes on the tellers, so a ringside seat, as it were. There are five windows but usually only two or three are manned, depending on the time of day. Technical is a little tricky and sound could be a challenge."

"And you will overcome this challenge how?"

For all his Southern charm, when it came down to business Powell was relentless. Stephen took it all in his stride, knowing him well enough to be ready with the answers.

"When Valentinova shows up we will have someone on foot in the line behind for audio and someone at the next window for video close up. Brad has kept two of his team away from the bank so they won't have been seen there before."

Stephen paused for questions, but none forthcoming he went on.

"Beta team, under Charlie, remember him from that Berlin thing?"

Powell nodded.

"Charlie's boys are on Valentinova. It's not quite so straightforward. Valentin knows his stuff and has a villa out of town on the Paphos Road. Double wire fence, dogs round the clock, two goons in tow every time she sets foot outside the compound, and technical a supermax prison governor back home would be proud of."

"However?"

Powell seemed to know instinctively that Stephen would already have worked out a solution.

Stephen was grinning from ear to ear, enjoying their sparring.

"However, Mrs. V has a weakness. A soft spot for her personal trainer Carlo. Fifteen years too young for her but he's the type to know money, need and opportunity when he sees it. The two of them pop off together after training in his little Alfa Romeo for lunch and a fuck in town somewhere, with the goons well and truly warned off. And guess what, she takes the chance while she's in the city to pop into the bank and launder some FSB money for herself before heading home to her watchers."

"Sweet."

"Sweet."

My English was rusty. Powell and Stephen sometimes used words I knew, but in different ways than I expected or could remember.

"What's she like?"

"Classic 'Type-A' personality, a real planner. She keeps a regular as clockwork schedule. We've managed to image her phone and downloaded her calendar. Tennis Monday, yacht club Wednesday and ex-pats on Friday, with Carlo, the post-gym workout and the bank on Tuesdays and Thursdays. She has nothing in the diary for Saturdays or Sundays. I guess she keeps those free to see her lovely husband now and then."

"Perfect. So tomorrow it's Carlo and then the bank."

"I'll bet you fifty bucks she is at the bank between one and two. Brad and his very keen lawyer have a meeting with the bank manager scheduled for tomorrow at twelve thirty. Only this time, they will be accompanied by his two bosses over from the Big Apple to keep an eye on things. That's you and Alexander. Thought you would want a front row seat."

Powell nodded in my direction.

Having failed to follow the Americans in full flow just now, I offered some advice.

"You had better do all the talking."

"Alexander, my friend, that won't be a problem."

21 VALENTINOVA

October 2

I had seen a hundred banks just like it. Admittedly, the quality of the fittings and wood counter looked better, and the surveillance cameras looked more modern compared to most back home, but otherwise just the same.

I took an instant dislike to the thin smarmy bank manager who greeted us individually like long lost family members before shepherding us into the conference room. The teller's windows were to the left.

The manager spoke good English, probably on account of the British being the resident launderers in chief in Cyprus before the Russians arrived. Powell averted an immediate crisis when the thin man went to close the blinds for privacy. Affecting a stronger Southern accent than usual, he would have none of it.

"No need for that now, we have no secrets from y'all,

let's enjoy the sunshine. Stephen would you run through the contract for Alexander and I?"

"In how much detail?"

"Thirty-thousand feet view is fine. We know you won't have missed a trick and it would be a shame to waste such a fine afternoon."

The bank manager sat down where Powell indicated and Stephen and our Cypriot lawyer boxed him in. Powell and I sat on the opposite side of the table with an unobstructed view of the bank customers coming and going.

Stephen opened his laptop and began a conversation that only the bank manager and the lawyer had any interest in. Knowing that the deal would meet his quarterly targets in one fell swoop the manager was all ears and paid Powell, me and the public outside not the least attention.

In my business, over the years I had learned to be a patient watcher. I didn't check my phone or pull my sleeve up to see my watch. Valentinova would get here, when she got here. Specifically, when she had finished with her lover boy for the day and not before. Powell was just as patient but somehow also managed to interject a couple of apparently relevant questions that engaged Stephen and the bank manager. He was a class act. Kislitsyn had chosen wisely when he picked someone from the American side.

For the umpteenth time I looked up, but it was the last. I caught her as soon as she walked in. From the pictures I had seen it was unmistakably Ludmilla Ellena Valentinova, even though the tight fitting sweat top and pants revealed a far more attractive figure than the surveillance photos gave her credit for.

I must have been staring a little too obviously. Powell, who continued to give all the appearance of being wholly involved in the negotiations, moved to cover my 'tell' with a question to distract anyone who may have noticed. I simply couldn't help it. I couldn't take my eyes off Valentin's unfaithful wife. It was as close as I had got to my friends' murderers so far.

In the line, the shabby old man before her concluded his business and moved on holding some bills tightly in his hand, perhaps to him a fortune. As Valentinova approached the counter I admired the tradecraft of Powell's team.

The sound quality of the earpieces Powell's man had fitted us with was excellent. I could hear every word and to prying eyes they looked just like digital hearing aids.

In the line at the next window to the Russian a middle-aged woman in a headscarf played the part of an annoying American complaining loudly to the teller. She was asking why in the hell she needed her passport to change a lousy two hundred bucks and demanding to see the manager. The target glanced at the unhappy customer, before turning back and dumping her purse on the counter.

"What can I do for you today Mrs. Valentinova?"

"Can you check that there were four deposits today?"

"One minute please."

It took no more than seconds.

"Yes, four deposits confirmed for this morning. All cleared. And will there be your usual transfer today?"

"Please. Wire the value of one of the deposits to the other account, the one for about nine hundred thousand dollars. And as usual make the transfer in Euros."

The teller typed at his keyboard calculating the exchange, then turned and removed a page from the printer.

"If you could please sign, I will complete the wire."

As the teller pushed a form through the gap in the window, the annoying American woman turned and tried to engage Valentinova in her complaint. In the few seconds in which she distracted both the target and the teller, the young man on a cell phone in the line behind moved his phone from his ear, as if to check a number. I just knew that as he did so he had snapped a photo or took a video of the transfer authorization, which was face up on the counter. It was that quick and that simple.

The complainant, to obvious relief, then found her passport in her purse and problem solved cancelled her demand to see the manager. She began fiddling with her phone, as the bank clerk inspected her passport.

Powell's phone buzzed on the table. He picked it up and read it, nodding a confirmation to me before he spoke.

"Excellent news. Head office has given the okay to proceed as per your proposal Stephen. Perhaps you could complete the final details and meet us for dinner later. I am dying to show Alexander that fish restaurant you told us about last night. We can sign the final contracts when they are drawn up tomorrow. Let's say, here at eleven, that good with everyone?"

The manager and the lawyer thought that was very good indeed. If he was in any way offended by the rudeness of our departure and being left with a junior partner, he disguised it as well as any good bank managers would.

"Tomorrow then."

We left the bank without another word, just catching sight of the rude American exiting and following her.

The café arranged as the meeting point was two blocks away. She walked straight on. By the time we had chosen a street side seat and ordered a glass of rosé the young man on the phone back at the bank was squeezing between our table and the next. As he headed for a seat, he accidently bumped the other table, briefly putting a hand on ours for balance. In one movement Powell picked up a menu and scooped up the phone he had left, putting it in his jacket pocket with the other hand. It remained there until the wine was served and the waiter retreated. He scrolled straight to the photos.

"Clear as a bell. Account number with Commercial Bank of Malta. An eight hundred and thirty thousand Euros transfer. That, my friend, is a nice little cut for Valentin. The spy business must be on the up."

Powell handed me the phone. Valentinova had a confident signature and a clear hand. Giving it back, he put his glasses on to get the numbers right in his text back home.

His other phone, still on the table, pinged. He read the text.

"Carlo has just dropped Ludmilla back at the villa."

We settled back to enjoy our wine, guzzling it in the excitement. Pouring us a second glass for ourselves, Stephen sauntered in and taking a seat, ordered himself a beer at the bar. With few people around he caught my eye and lifted his glass in our direction, no doubt delighted that his plan had gone like clockwork.

"Your man looks happy with the way things went."

"I expected nothing else. He is one of my top men."

"Now Alexander, there is nothing for us old spooks to do but enjoy our lunch, while the owls keep watch on the targets and the geeks back home type bank details into whatever databases they can steal access to. Stephen will keep an eye on things."

"That is, as you American guys say, a real shame."

Powell drained his glass and waved in the direction of the hovering waiter. With him for company and his team nearby, for the first time for what seemed an age I felt like I could chill out. The wine was helping.

"Tell me how you ended up working for the KGB. You seem too darn nice a gentleman for that."

"Only if you tell me how you came to be with such an evil organization as the Agency first."

"It's a deal. As for me, no mystery really. Do you read fiction Alexander?"

He continued before I could answer.

"Anyway, I love it, pure escapism. My favorite author,

an Englishman, ex-spook himself, has portrayed the vocation for people like us, who look deep into men's souls for a living, as being a choice between priest or spy. I found I didn't have the depth of deception required for the priesthood."

I burst out laughing. It was hard not to like Powell. I told him the story of my father and how I followed him into the family business.

I felt relaxed. Not just because of the wine and bonhomie, but because deep down I knew we were making progress towards getting to Kislitsyn and Kirilov's murderers. And I knew what I would do when we got there.

22 DEAL

After my afternoon snooze back at the hotel I took a walk to get some fresh air and shake off the boozy lunch with Powell. For an American he could hold his drink, but then again, he had spent a lot of time over the years in Moscow.

Stephen had taken it easy, knowing full well that was his role as the junior man and being responsible for supervising the surveillance teams. After a few drinks I had teased him about not sharing the CIA official Op name, but as he insisted there was no need for me to know and despite being a cooperating asset, I didn't have the appropriate clearance. Their trust had limits.

Refreshed I met Powell and Stephen for dinner. Choosing a quiet corner table in the hotel restaurant we set about planning the next day's surveillance. Unlike lunch dinner was all business, most of it a detailed discussion about the individuals in the surveillance teams and the logistics of their specific duties for the big day. I didn't know them or the 'lay of the land' as Powell called it, so I kept quiet.

The main locations we would have eyes on remained the villa and the bank. Tomorrow was expected to be a long day. We planned constant surveillance on Valentinova, ready to catch and record any indiscretion, particularly sleeping with the help or stealing Russian Government money. A little jaded from earlier, once the planning was done Powell and I headed for an early night.

I spent an uneventful evening watching TV, falling asleep, fully clothed, with the set still on. I eventually climbed under the covers at two in the morning.

Now I couldn't sleep. It was always like this with me the night before a mission, wide awake at all hours, focused only on what could go wrong. I recalled that saying Kislitsyn had picked up in his time abroad, 'whatever could go wrong, would go wrong.' He had drilled into me to plan for all the eventualities you thought possible, but on top of that, to be flexible and expect the unexpected. Nine times out of ten, it worked out, allowing you to believe you had thought of everything. The other times, though, were usually a cluster fuck, that could cost you, your asset, or both, their lives.

*　　　　　*　　　　　*

October 3

I was up and ready early, eager to just get going. But there was nothing I could do to speed things up. Valentinova's schedule dictated everything, leaving me an increasingly edgy wait.

As planned, spot on ten Powell and I began making our way down the crowded high street. Locals and tourists mixed on the narrow sidewalks, dipping in and out of the shops and cafés. We had dressed down at Stephen's request. He told us the observation point was more of a blue-collar local's place than a tourist trap.

Powell provided a hooded top that more or less fitted. It had 'Alabama Crimson Tide' emblazoned on it, which he said was his college football team. He joked that he would make a Southern gentleman out of me if it killed him. I told him I very much imagined it would. He had not shaved since yesterday, thick grey stubble aging him, despite the trendy clothes and Yankees baseball cap Stephen had foisted on him.

The café door was propped open to let in the sea breeze and help the struggling ceiling fan. Stephen had claimed the one table in the bay window and had an inviting pot of hot coffee waiting. As soon as he we had poured mugs he began. Today he seemed as anxious as I was to get going.

"It's the building opposite. Second floor, corner window on the right, with the balcony and window boxes. She's in. We have a camera in the corridor covering the front door, one guy on a motorbike in the side street in case there is traffic and a car round the back, on the off chance she skips out that way."

Stephen had said all he had to say and this time without questions from Powell or I, we settled down to wait. For once we were in luck. I noticed the young American stop as he poured himself another cup and put his forefinger to his ear, although I couldn't see an earpiece. He slammed the mug down.

"She's walking out the back now. Making a left turn. Dressed up, blue suit, cream blouse, heels. We can shadow her down the High Street, this road is more or less parallel."

"Come on Alexander, let's go."

I didn't need asking twice.

We walked at the leisurely pace set by Stephen, presumably based on what he was getting in his earpiece from the watchers. He relayed anything important.

"Copy. She has let a couple of empty cabs go by so it seems she is set on walking. The boys think she could be heading for the Marina. Valentin has a brand spanking new French built yacht moored there, thirty-footer."

Powell and I shared a knowing look. Valentin was turning the money he was creaming off the Russian Intelligence Services into real assets for a rainy day. I doubted they knew about the new yacht back at Moscow Center. Another detail we could threaten Valentin with disclosing.

Stephen stopped to look at the window display of a shoe shop. This time he didn't touch the earpiece but I was somehow sure he was getting a message from the watchers.

Powell had stopped too, seemingly admiring a painting in the window of a quaint shop on the opposite side of the road. When I joined him, he said it was the artists choice of color that impressed him. Stephen crossed the street to admire another painting in the next window.

"She has gone into Armani. If she still heads for the marina when she comes out, we could get ahead of her and box the square for the watchers."

Powell nodded his ascent.

"OK, take the next right, then the first left and you will be on the same street as her, where most of the fancy stores are, but about two hundred yards ahead, walking towards the seafront. I'll get ahead of you now and find a bar or café ready for a switch. I will text you the name and location."

There was no shortage of designer shops in Cyprus these days, ready and waiting to relieve their rich Russian customers of their hard-laundered money.

Stephen walked on, while Powell returned to admiring the painting. Apparently, he liked not only the colors but also the way the artist captured the light reflecting off the water. To the disappointment of the shop keeper who had come out to serve us, he told him that much as he liked the picture it was way out of his price range.

Ambling across to the sunnier side of the street we followed in Stephen's direction. Powell was dawdling and I think sensed I was keen to press on. It must have been obvious to him that I couldn't wait to get my eyes on Valentinova in person, to stay close to one of those involved in the conspiracy that ended up with my boss and my young colleague dead.

"Don't hurry Alexander. Ludmilla won't be rushing her shopping and Stephen and the watchers are more than a match for her, even if she is a trained spook."

"She's in the business too? That's something else I didn't know."

"Was, but you never really leave the KGB, right? They

can always come calling. Valentin met her at Yasenevo. He was teaching, although our intelligence isn't good enough to tell us what KGB skullduggery he was espousing. She never completed her training."

That may have been years ago, but she would not have forgotten all she learned. The endless days and months of repetitive practice, how could you forget that? It became second nature and in time it became you. You simply didn't remember you were doing something you didn't do before, that ordinary people didn't do at all.

Powell paused in an alleyway alongside a baker's shop and discreetly put his earpiece back in. Stephen kept us in the loop as the target dragged her watchers from one store to another. Stopping regularly at designer shop windows, she was either on the lookout for something new or double-checking reflections for a tail. Instinct told me it was the latter. Stephen's investment in a double team for the surveillance could pay off. If there had been one team they could have been blown, but given Ludmilla's rustiness and lack of actual field experience there was no way she could keep track of two full teams of seasoned watchers.

Then she made her move. She settled down for a coffee at an outside table on a street corner café. As the waiter walked away having served her espresso Ludmilla shoved a banknote under the saucer and made off on foot without taking so much as a sip. Anyone who had settled and now had to get straight up to follow could have been blown.

Stephen's team must have sensed that she was going to make a move sooner rather than later, after a parade of shops where she bought nothing. They must have kept their distance, albeit keeping her boxed in. He calmly relayed their messages. She was walking quickly and was about to catch up with one of the forward watchers when she stopped abruptly and walked into a street corner building.

"She has just walked into a branch of the Cyprus Popular Credit Bank. We haven't come across this before."

Powell said that he had never heard of it, but Stephen spoke up.

"It's been through a few mergers over the last few years following the latest Cypriot and Greek banking crisis. Has a sketchy reputation, and there are rumors of significant Russian involvement. This could be what we were looking for."

Powell and I listened to his concise orders.

"Confirmed. Follow her in. Light touch. We don't want to spook her."

Ludmilla was no more than five minutes in the bank.

"The watcher says she knew the cashier. First name terms, so this looks a regular stop. They couldn't get close enough to hear any details, the branch was half empty and the other teller was too far away."

"Suggestions?"

Powell was looking at me but I think the question was for the team. Stephen replied before anyone else had chance and as usual didn't mention names when I was listening.

"As we are short on time, I suggest the watcher who was in the bank and I focus on the teller who seems familiar with Valentinova. We could approach him with financial inducement for a little financial intelligence. I could play the Interpol card, telling him we are following drug cartel money and want to keep a low profile as we suspect the local authorities are being paid off to keep a blind eye. That said, we have a budget for cooperative witnesses. They usually want to help fight the good fight against the drug gangs, especially if they get a little reward for their public service. What do you think?"

"Works for me. You two make the approach. Alexander and I will go back to the hotel Ops room. No need to risk anyone being able to describe me and my Russian friend here to anyone asking difficult questions later."

"It won't be long. The banks here close at two thirty. Oh, and they don't do Fridays."

"Jesus, they are just as bad as the Greeks. No wonder they are bankrupt."

*   *   *

Stephen called just after four. Powell greeted him but headed out to the balcony for the call. I guess out of habit he maintained a distrust of foreign hotel rooms. He wasn't out there for long.

"That was Stephen. They got a result with the teller. He was a little reluctant at first, citing bank regulations and the existence of a formal process to get the information they wanted. But he was more helpful when shown Interpol credentials and told they suspected drug cartels were the source of Valentinova's deposits. More talkative again, when he added they didn't need specific bank account details and respected client confidentiality, bank secrecy rules and all that. All they wanted was a rough idea of the routes the money was going so we could speed up formal bank information requests through official channels to those jurisdictions. The teller told him the money went to accounts in London and New York. Surprise, surprise. What dodgy Russian spy or crook wouldn't want to keep their money there, safely out of Putin's grasp. It makes sense."

"Agreed. That's where I would put it. And I'd maybe hide it in real estate there too. Half of the property in Manhattan and Mayfair is Russian owned now."

"Stephen got enough out of the teller to know that the wire transfers were through business accounts, not personal ones, and that they took place every other Wednesday, regular as clockwork. Each time Ludmilla comes into the branch to conduct the transactions. Hence, he knew her to talk to. So, we have the destination."

"How so?"

"It won't take our friends back home long to isolate big money wires, only conducted every other Wednesday, from accounts at the Cyprus Popular Credit Bank to London and New York financial institutions. And, of course, we know they can't involve businesses who wired money more than say a year ago. The scheme hasn't been going that long, judging by when the teller told us Ludmilla first showed up."

"Just like that."

"Yep, just like that. We will have it all by the time we wake up tomorrow. So now we can move to the next phase of the Op."

"Which is?"

"You're not going to like this Alexander but I want you to stay here and monitor events from the hotel with Stephen. I am going back to Moscow tonight to make the pitch to Valentin."

"No fucking way. This is my investigation. I want that bastard. I want that bastard's head!"

Powel spoke quietly but firmly. His voice carried authority.

"That's exactly why you can't go. He knows that only too well. Besides it's way too dangerous. We got you out by the skin of your teeth and by now your photo will be at every border crossing from St. Petersburg to Vladivostok. It's too risky and we haven't got the time to build a complete cover for you and get you back undetected."

I knew he was right. But I didn't like it one bit. And I had other doubts.

"He won't go for it. He will never work with Americans. He may be a crook like the rest of them, but he is an ultra-nationalist. He hates America more than you can imagine and he won't give you anything against the President or his inner circle."

"In which case you won't be missing anything. I have to try though, Alexander. Langley wants this watertight before we go to the White House with evidence and recommendations for additional sanctions. At the same time, the top floor argues we have got Valentin over a barrel, so we will never have a better chance to turn him and get back a top source in the Kremlin. It's public knowledge that we had to pull the last one after that blabbermouth in the Oval Office burned him by leaking information, we received in strictest confidence from Israel, about an active ISIS plot."

"I read that in the papers."

"But if it is as you say, and he won't be turned, then we will throw him to the wolves. With the thugs who are running things there now, he's as good as dead. They can't risk him talking to anyone in future and more important they have to send a message about what happens to people who steal from them."

For all my hothead reputation, as I got older, I had learned not to make big decisions when I was angry. Smash the place up a little, rough up a scumbag prisoner or go on an all-night bender. But don't make important decisions when you are boiling. I knew if I was picked up entering the country and they got to work on me, it would tip off Valentin before Powell and the Agency could get hold of him. And besides, even if I got through border checks Valentin's bodyguards wouldn't let me get within a hundred yards of him. Then I remembered the old ladies on the bus and Powell's view before our first meeting.

"And if I stay, I can monitor the pitch from here? When you threaten to expose his theft, I need to see him squirm."

"You will be able to see and hear every word, I promise. I'll have the technical people set cameras up and patch a live-feed back to Langley and the Ops room here. This goes all the way to the top. Valentin is as high profile as it gets back home, the hottest ticket in town. They want a front row seat too. You will have as good a view as the Director of the CIA and the White House. Deal?"

"Deal."

We shook on it. It was a fair bargain. It would be just plain rude to demand a better view than the American President or head of the CIA, wouldn't it?

23 PITCH

October 4

Stephen sent one of the boys to collect me from my room before I had finished my breakfast. There was an update from Langley. When I got to the Ops room, he was typing away at one of the computers.

"We got a cable from Langley. They identified a second OSA account for UKRAINImport. They have traced the outgoing funds from there and they go via a Turkish company and finish up in Donbass, Ukraine."

"What's an OSA account?"

"OSA means Over-Seas Account. On the East Europe desk at Langley they have been busy boys and girls. They tell me they have leveraged the Ukrainian intelligence service to share an asset of theirs so they can trace the end of the money chain. It seems the Ukrainian service has a reliable journalist in the Donbass area who was able to bribe someone in the bank. I love bank people, with them everything has a price, loyalty, privacy, information, whatever. Anyhow, the bank guy has tipped the asset off about the local militia collection, bulk cash, every Friday. The Ukrainians aren't hanging around and they have an Op set up for this week, to get some nice photos of the little green men carting off Valentin's Russian Federation payroll. They are more than happy to pass any intelligence on to us, in anticipation we will do something about it and the opposition payroll dries up."

"So now you have everything. The complete money trail from Russian Intelligence Services property sales, through shell companies in the UK and Cyprus, to banks in East Ukraine, and cash collections there to pay Russian backed fighters."

"Yep, and after we get the pictures of the cash collection by the bad guys, every step documented too. The Ukrainian intelligence folks, being the very diligent types of spies that they are, also promised that after they get their photos of the cash collection, they will use their journalist to blackmail the bank source. I have no doubt he will get them copies of the bank statements too, with a very real threat to be given up to the Russian-backed hoods hanging over him if he doesn't."

"And Powell has enough to pitch Valentin?"

"He has more than enough. His plane landed in Moscow a few hours ago. Take a seat, the show is about to start."

*   *   *

As he brought the live-feed up on the monitor Stephen told me Powell had arranged to meet Valentin somewhere public, somewhere neutral, somewhere neither would be known. The Starlite Diner in downtown Moscow fitted the bill. A chintzy cartoon version created in the nineties of how the American diner looked in corny movies back in the fifties. After Gorbachev in the infant short-lived freedoms of post-Soviet Russia everything American was cool. Maybe the diner, like the freedom, even felt real for a while.

The picture switched to a camera showing Powell walking in, close behind two of his smartly dressed bodyguards, who were doing their best to pretend not to know him. Some of Powell's advance team were scattered about the diner in various degrees of scruffiness.

He picked a booth in the middle of the room, by a window and next to a life-size Elvis Presley poster. The picture was from long before the iconic singer had gotten fat, and the background looked like Hawaii.

A waitress came up to him. Stephen was fiddling with the sound, which so far was not cooperating.

There were plenty of other serious looking characters hanging around, no doubt Valentin's men among them. The couple I picked out first seemed from the empty plates and half-finished coffee cups in front of them to have been there as long as the Americans. I was checking out another one when his sudden disinterest in the newspaper he was holding and complete focus toward the entrance confirmed I was right and Valentin's arrival.

Powell obviously felt need to be discreet and turned and watched the Russian General's entrance. Although the picture flickered when the agency man moved it was clear enough to see Valentin's stomp into the diner. An expression of annoyance at the uninvited intrusion of the

Americans.

At last with one me bash on the keyboard the sound came on. Stephen was on my left and in charge, with Brad, one of the surveillance team leaders crowding in from my right.

The picture shifted to one from an agent closer to where Powell was sitting. I could clearly hear Powell stirring his coffee. Valentin came into shot as sat down on the bench seat directly opposite Powell. Valentin waved and I caught the bulk of two of his bodyguards move off camera, presumably to find a seat nearby.

"*Dobryy vecher.*"

"What do you want Mr. Powell. I have no time for your games and cryptic messages."

"General Valentin I am far too old for games. Let me speak plainly. We know about the whole operation, from the property sales in Moscow to the murders of Kislitsyn and Kirilov. We are fully aware of Highland East Europe Enterprises, we know all about the role of UKRAINImport, the extent of the Cyprus money laundering and the bankrolling of the militia in Crimea and East Ukraine with the proceeds. We have the bank account details, the documentary proof, the lot."

Valentin didn't flinch. He sat motionless for what seemed an age. The tension was broken by the appearance of the waitress, only partly in shot, asking if he wanted a coffee.

"*Nyet*"

His stare didn't budge from Powell. The waitress shot off.

"I don't know what you are talking about Mr. Powell and I have work to do."

Valentin got up to go, but Powell grabbed his arm.

"Your wife checks on the FSB accounts every Thursday and wires about twenty percent of the total to a secret account you two have at the Cyprus Popular Credit Bank. I guess the scam is you tell Moscow Center it costs forty percent to reliably wash their money, when in reality it costs half that, and you keep the difference. Clever, but very, very, risky."

Valentin sat back down. It was hard to see but, in my mind at least, I imagined he had gone very pale. I heard a 'gotcha' from one of the off-duty watchers straining for a view behind us.

Valentin produced a packet of cigarettes and a lighter and lit one, without offering one to Powell. He took a long heavy drag.

"As I said Mr. Powell, what is it you want?"

"Personally, I want you tried for the murder of your colleagues, but Langley, who have bigger fish to fry, would very much like you to leave with me for the Baltic and to give them chapter and verse on the whole scheme, including the names of those in the President's inner circle that are involved. The U.S. Government can protect you and the compensation would be substantial."

Valentin took another long drag, killing time. Time to think.

"And why on earth would I do that? I am not a sniveling traitor like the Kislitsyn man you recruited."

The bastard couldn't even bring himself to mention me by

name.

"Why? Because, financial compensation aside, if you don't, we will give up to the media worldwide your involvement in theft from the Russian State and their illegal financing of the militia in Ukraine. That to go along with news of the new, deep and wide sanctions we will be imposing on additional members of the inner circle, their companies and their banks. I would have thought that would not go down too well with your bosses or the President's cronies."

Valentin said nothing. He just carried on smoking.

Powell lifted his coffee cup to signal the waitress back.

She topped up his coffee with a smile, ignoring the other man.

"I am going to finish my coffee. You have until then to decide whether you want to live out a comfortable life in safety, somewhere warm, with your wife for company. Or if the two of you would rather face the wrath of your superiors and their henchmen, like Ivanov from the good old days of Department V, for instance?"

Smart of Powell to mention Valentinova and Ivanov in his pitch. The Russian may have been the brave soldier ready to die for his country, even at its own hand, but even he would surely think twice about subjecting his wife to anything that psycho could dream up.

I stared at Valentin's cold emotionless face. It reminded me what a ruthless bastard he was. No, he wouldn't care about saving his wife. He wouldn't bat an eyelid. And if he found out about Carlo, he'd pull the trigger himself, probably only after having them both beaten senseless first.

Before Powell had taken a second swig, Valentin leaned towards him, his voice a whisper.

"You fucking Americans. You think you can waltz into my backyard, my homeland, and tell me what to do. Those days are over. Whether I live or die is not important. What is important is that we have Crimea, we have its navy base, we have Donbass, and we have a strong President who is rebuilding our army, our navy and our air force. We will build a wedge between Turkey and you and destroy the NATO conspiracy against us, leaving the whole of demilitarized, flabby, impotent Western Europe at our mercy, to take if and when we want."

Valentin stood up, turned and went to go.

Powell did not bother to keep his voice down.

"Don't kid yourself Valentin. You serve a criminal gang running a country, not even the other way round, and that never ends well. You are a fool to die for it, and a heartless bastard to leave your wife to face the consequences of your greed."

Valentin made no response, walking casually towards the exit, as if he didn't have a care in the world. He was not going to give Powell the satisfaction of seeing him scurrying away to make good his escape. If he planned to run that is. The picture blinked twice, then went blank.

"Well, there it is. You were right Alexander, there was no way he was going to go for it. And now you have got what you wanted. That is a dead man walking".

"Not a man. A coward and a murderer heading for death

row. Nobody has ever deserved it more."

24 LANGLEY

Stephen told me he was going to pick Powell up at the airport on his return to Cyprus and asked me to come along. I expected a late night but he told me the flight time was just four hours or so and as there was no time difference between Moscow and Cyprus that wouldn't be the case.

As we drove the American filled me in. Powell left Moscow by private jet soon after his meeting at the diner. He had cabled Langley to confirm what they already knew, that Valentin was determined to go down with the ship. Having confronted and pitched the General his usefulness in his current mission as a military attaché on behalf of the Director of National Intelligence was over. There was now every chance the Russian's would choose to expose his connections to the CIA before expelling him from the country.

Stephen drove right onto the edge of the runway as the small plane came in to land. We got out and stood on the apron, waiting for it to taxi back. It was hard to believe he had left yesterday, taken a return trip to Moscow, tried to recruit an FSB General and was back in time for cocktails and dinner. The Agency moved quickly. If that had been my old department running a similar operation, to pitch a senior CIA officer inside US borders, it could have taken months.

Contrary to popular myth, Moscow Center was very considered, if not cautious in the extreme, when it came to recruiting new agents. Everything was by the book, and the book had been written a long time ago. The KGB had been so paranoid about being infiltrated, in the same way they had targeted MI5 and MI6, that when Philby and the Cambridge Five delivered their gold-standard intelligence many in Moscow Center, for years, believed it was too good to be true and dismissed it all as a British double agent ploy.

The deafening engines of the jet-black unmarked jet looming up in front of us put a stop to my contemplations. As soon as it came to a halt the ground crew were opening the rear door. Powell bounded down the stairs.

"All change. Langley has just ordered us to pitch the wife tomorrow. To see if we can get anything from her and make up for what they are describing as our failure in Moscow."

"Wow boss, they are not letting it go, are they?"

"Fuck no, they're not. I guess the White House is piling the pressure on and the top floor are too scared to say no to the bully boy in the Oval Office. Spineless, pen-pushing, bureaucratic, cowards to a man."

"And woman."

Powell smiled.

"Whatever the politics, gender or otherwise, it'll be us hung out to dry if we screw it up tomorrow."

Driving back the Powell and Stephen got into the planning in detail. I was curious.

"Why did your bosses change tack all of a sudden?"

"After I told them about Valentin's refusal to play ball they started asking about his marriage, throwing questions about Valentinova and Carlo's relationship. I guess they see a genuine opportunity there. To be fair Valentinova may know more than we think she does. Ultimately, they focused on her being an ex-KGB operative. They seem to think she will take what you might call a pragmatic approach."

"I don't know her. Maybe she is not like Valentin. It could be worth a try."

"Stephen, can you get everything we discussed set up in time for tomorrow?"

He smiled, exuding confidence.

"Sure. The teams are in place and we have her pattern of life down to a tee. Tomorrow morning is shopping in the town center. We could easily approach her when she takes her break for lunch. She usually eats alone from what we have seen. That would be the perfect chance."

"Has Valentin warned her?"

"That we don't know for sure. Not via the phones the NSA has ears on, for certain, but by other means, who knows?

"Alexander what do you think?"

"I don't think he will have done. He is an arrogant controlling prick, and I don't think he would want Valentinova to think for a moment he has been out maneuvered."

"Good point. Then, what's his play?"

"I think he will wait for you Americans to make the first move. He will want to see exactly what you do, before he does anything at all. You told him you know all about Valentinova and specifically mentioned the Cyprus Popular Credit Bank. To him the accounts there are blown and they won't be his priority now. In my opinion his priorities will be twofold. One, making safe the funds in the accounts and assets we didn't mention, the yacht for instance. And two, the actions he predicts his superiors will take. He will be working to call in all the favors he can to save his fortune and his skin."

"Like it, thank you Alexander, that's helpful. Right, Stephen in the circumstances that's not the worst plan. Let's get on with it. Our media liaison is going to leak the 'Russian Militia funded through London and Cyprus shell companies' story to the Wall Street Journal and New York Times tomorrow, around noon, our time. So, we will have the chance to pitch Valentinova in the early afternoon, before the papers get the story up and running."

"And the sanctions story, who is running with that?"

"I wanted TV for that so CNN and NBC news will get that a few hours later. We will leak something to the effect of 'senior government sources advise of a new round of

Ukraine linked sanctions against Russian owned and funded banks in Cyprus'. That should get some airtime."

"If Valentinova doesn't believe us from the start, the new sanctions and Russian militia stories should attract her attention. And how about showing her a portion of the video from your pitch to her husband yesterday? Boss, that should focus her mind on her immediate future."

"Agreed, that would be perfect. Now, trying to recruit Russian spies has worn me out. I want something to eat then a good night's sleep."

This time we were all in the same SUV. Powell got in the front and closed his eyes right away. I heard Stephen call Brad to get the surveillance guys to order pizza for us before I dozed off myself.

Back at the hotel everything was set up on Powell's balcony. There was nothing proper for a real Russian to drink but I was getting used to the wine the guys had a liking for. They told me the 'Nero D'Avola' they had stuck to was from Sicily rather than Cyprus. Brad joked that as he was the one doing the expenses, he liked it because it was cheap.

After a few minutes the surveillance guys left the three of us to talk. They had eaten fast, as people always on the move do. And, from experience, they also knew that as their flights out had been put on hold, we had another phase of the Op to discuss.

We went over the plan in detail, then that we relaxed. After a lot of pushing and a few glasses of red, Powell gave in to Stephen and I and agreed to tell us more about his meeting with Valentin.

"He was just as cold as you described Alexander. I have met KGB Generals like him before. But back then, I could at least understand they were like they were because they were mostly true believers, convinced in the inevitability of Western betrayal and that we were out to destroy them from the first day after the Revolution. With some in the Pentagon and Whitehouse over the years they weren't all that wrong. But now with Valentin's generation, it is just crude criminality hiding behind Russian nationalism."

"Where did he go after the diner?"

"The watchers told me he went straight back to his mansion. We have it under surveillance twenty-four, seven."

"Did he have any visitors?"

"None so far. He increased his security detail that night. I am told they are FSB guards, but known to be loyal to Valentin personally. They have been with him for years."

"And he made no attempt to leave Moscow?"

"No, no change to his routine at all. He was back at Yasenevo the next morning as though nothing had happened."

"He is too proud to run."

"Stephen, any thoughts?"

"One more thing. Valentin is playing it cool. If he sticks to his normal routine, doesn't panic, and keeps everything normal, then when confronted he could argue that the whole Cyprus twenty percent cut story is an

American plot. He will say it is just a CIA attempt to discredit him. That would play for a while and buy him some time to finalize escape plans and get his cash away, with or without Valentinova".

"Yes, that makes sense. He is a cool customer. Would that be your view Alexander?"

The Valentin I knew, a survivor of the dirtiest and worst campaigns in Chechnya, who escaped Grozny without a blot on his record as intelligence chief, despite Russian loses, he knew how to keep his cool. He would always have alternatives, including an escape plan for emergencies.

"I agree with Stephen. What he said is entirely feasible."

"But what does that mean for our Op plan for tomorrow?"

"I don't see a problem with our plan, we just need to bring it forward and execute it as soon as possible. The news leaks need to be tonight. We need to alert Valentin's bosses that he is stealing their money before he has any time to make good his escape."

Powell thought about what Stephen had said for a moment.

"Excuse me gentlemen, but I need to cable Langley."

As he stood to leave, he must have noticed the widening smile on my face.

"Alexander, is something amusing you?"

"Valentin thinks he has increased his bodyguard, but in reality, he has just doubled his own jailers. And by tonight he will know he is under house arrest."

25 SNATCHED

October 5

Powell, Stephen and I picked up surveillance of Valentinova outside the mansion. She had ordered a taxi rather than allow one of the guards to drive her, so we suspected the usual liaison with Carlo was on the cards.

With traffic on the light side it was easy to keep tabs on her from a safe distance. Just to be on the safe side we rotated with the other two surveillance cars. She surprised us and took the main road to Limassol, which was busier, meaning we could close up a little. It looked like a day's shopping at the seaside was her choice for today. Poor Carlo would have to wait.

"Stephen, run through our options for the approach one more time."

Stephen was driving, but had no trouble taking the phone from its cradle on the dashboard with one hand.

Handing it back to us, he got Powell to open the CNN news app. Headlining was news of proposed new sanctions against Russia.

"Our best option is to be direct, show her the sanctions story and let her know her liberty and safety are at immediate risk. We can offer to provide her with protection in return for a simple statement. Nothing major, at first anyway, just an explanation of the money trail and what the whole scheme is about. And we want it in writing."

"Agreed. That's the 'why, who and what.' Give me your thinking for the 'when, where and how?'"

"From what we know Valentinova almost always takes lunch alone when she is out shopping, usually at a high-end restaurant. That would be a better choice than an approach on the street, which is too public, or one of those boutique shops, which are often too quiet to talk. We had better steer well clear of the mansion with Valentin's guards skulking about."

"Alexander?"

"I would choose the restaurant. And, not wanting to be pushy, but I should do the talking. I think a surprise unsolicited approach by an American would put her on the defensive. She is KGB trained after all and I am sure Valentin reminds her what to do in the event of uninvited foreign contact."

"That makes sense. Stephen, you keep your distance. Lunchtime approach it is, with Alexander taking the lead."

"Copy that. I'll make sure I get a good vantage point for video. I will set you up for sound."

Valentinova's taxi pulled up at the end of the street. We drove on fifty yards or so to a small car park near the seafront. Brad's surveillance team kept eyes on the target and were updating Stephen. We couldn't risk taking our eyes off her for a split second. Today would be our only chance and as Powell said when he briefed the watchers, Langley would lose its's shit if they thought we fucked this up like the pitch to the General.

Stephen headed off on foot and we followed, probably more closely than we should. After a couple of hundred yards he stopped to look in a shop window. The more I watched him, the more I realized he had a habit of stopping when he was trying to hear a message. Powell and I stopped close on either side of him when we caught up, eager for an update.

"She is working her way down the high street. They are saying she is ploughing ahead. It looks like she is not bothering with any anti-surveillance, like the trick before the last visit to the bank. I guess Valentin warned her to be extra careful when she went anywhere near their personal bank and bank account. When we followed her the other day, she was probably more on the lookout for FSB watchers than she was for the likes of us."

"How long do you reckon before she stops for lunch?"

"Could be an hour or two if she sticks to her usual schedule. She is a creature of habit, as we have seen. I would guess she would choose a restaurant between the castle and the marina for lunch. There are a lot of the better places to eat, there and thereabouts. And she does like the best of the best."

"In that case Alexander and I will take a break. There is

no point in us all hanging about here. Call me the minute she looks like she is done shopping and heading for lunch. And Stephen?"

"What?"

"Don't screw the pooch."

"Take a load off, we got this. We have Brad and our best people covering her every move and they are updating me, real time. I will call you the moment she looks like she is moving south. Why don't you guys take a look at the castle, I hear it's pretty cool and it's like five minutes from here, max."

Powell walked ahead down the narrow street. I sensed he wanted to give Stephen some space and himself some time to think.

I caught him by the walls. He began telling the castle was a lot smaller than he imagined it would be, not really fit for a King. Legend has it that this was where Richard the Lionheart had married his bride in the twelfth century, a princess from Navarre, who had, by the marriage, become Queen of England. He pushed on. Following him up the stone steps, I left him to his thoughts. I was out of breath when we made the battlements. From there we had a great view of the old harbor and the promenade. I had given him enough time.

"What was that with Stephen back there? You starting to feel the strain too?"

"You don't know the half of it. In the videoconference this morning that asshole Deputy Director asked the Director if he didn't think I was a little too old for a field Op of this importance. Fucking desk jockey. I was running

Ops when he was in kindergarten, the sniveling little shit. Two overseas postings in the hotbeds behind the lines that are Tokyo and London and he has the audacity to question my ability to run this show."

It was clear he needed the walk to calm down more than anything. We returned back down the steps, out onto the promenade.

"The bosses in Russia are the same. The ones who play it safe, do their headquarters time and don't get their hands dirty in risky overseas operations, they are the ones who make it to the top. No chances taken, no danger of mistakes. The grey men of the flabby bureaucracies we work for. Look at Putin, one lousy posting in East Germany spying on our own comrades."

"Some things never change my friend, the joy of working in the second oldest profession in the world."

He was smiling.

The phone rang and put a stop to that.

"She looks like she is heading to lunch. Stephen said he will catch us up on Athinon, that's a street just south of the market square."

When I saw Stephen on the corner ahead, drinking his Starbucks, I checked my watch. We had been walking bang on five minutes. He caught sight of us, dumped his takeaway cup and came straight over.

"Follow me back across the street and find a good spot. She is headed directly this way."

We kept about twenty yards behind. We didn't want

Valentinova to see us together, but we wanted to make sure we didn't lose him. The streets were filling up as lunchtime approached.

Tailing Stephen around a corner, I caught sight of her on the right side of the street, walking away from us, another ten yards on from him. We picked our pace up to keep eyes on.

Even before we closed on him, I heard the screech of tires. A black Mercedes pulled out from a side street alongside the target. For a second, she hesitated, but an imposing figure in a blue suit approached her from the sidewalk and grabbed her shopping bags out of her hand. He held the car door open. She knew she had no choice. Our watchers hadn't spotted anyone trailing her and I had seen how good they were. The only way, was if there was a tracker on her. Pointlessly, I wondered if they had known about Carlo all along.

The Merc started off slowly but accelerated as it turned down the next side street away from the crowds. A noisy two-stroke motorbike narrowly avoided us and zoomed round the same corner, leaving a trail of black smoke and scattered pedestrians behind.

We ran up to Stephen.

"Can you hear him?"

I guessed Powell was asking about the motorcyclist.

"Yep."

Silence.

Then Stephen spoke again.

"Roger. They are headed for the docks."

Powell and I kept close, in the hope of relayed messages. Another Op in a shared, long, litany of failed missions had gone to rat shit in an instant.

Each moment of silence seemed an age.

"Copy. Out."

Stephen turned to us, ashen faced.

"They sped through a side gate at the docks without slowing. The barrier crashed down behind and the port guards waved our tail to a halt. Wisely he backed off before they could ask any difficult questions."

We began walking back to the car in silence. All the while, I was wondering if that asshole Deputy Director was already crowing about how right he was when he said Powell was over the hill.

26 THE LIMAN

Stephen reversed the car out of the parking space at speed, skillfully avoiding a scooter rider, who gave him the finger. He didn't seem to notice.

"Our man has climbed a hill opposite to get a good view of the docks. He is looking to get a fix on the car."

Powell, in the front seat next to him, grabbed the phone and got the motorcyclist's exact location. At the illegal speed we were going it would only be a few minutes before we got there.

Getting out of the car it seemed quite a way from the harbor. A footpath led directly uphill from the road. Stephen fetched binoculars from the glove compartment and we headed up. It wasn't easy going, my knees complaining from the start. The young American pressed ahead, but Powell held back, I think to protect my feelings as much as anything else. Half way up, faking that I had forgotten he was a nonsmoker, I offered him a cigarette as an excuse for a rest. A picture of calm, he laid on his most gentlemanly southern accent and theatrically declined. He must have really been feeling the pressure but you would never know. He waited for me to light up before we carried on.

Where the path next crossed the road snaking up the hill, a low wall surrounded a few parking spaces, setback for people to take in the panoramic view. Limassol's commercial harbor was on our immediate left. Further on was a military airport. Powell noticed it had got my attention.

"RAF Akrotiri. Technically part of the United Kingdom. It has been a key base for them in the Mediterranean since the Suez crisis. Before the current Administration, when we still had a serious alliance against ISIS in Iraq and Syria, the Brits launched air support missions from there."

History lesson over he turned to Stephen who had been huddled with the watcher and filled him in.

"He has seen no sign of the Mercedes."

"Any ship movements?"

"A couple of fishing boats have arrived, but nothing bigger than a canoe has departed."

Stephen kept watch through the binoculars while Powell and I got as comfortable as we could sitting on the wall. I lit another cigarette and offered it to the watcher who, job done, had joined us. Like many in his trade would, he gratefully accepted. Smoking was very much part of my routine to kill time on surveillance job. Turning against the wind to try and light mine, Stephen spoke up before I succeeded.

"A ship is pulling away from the quay. It's not a trawler, looks like a small freighter of some kind. All grey, no shipping line on the hull, could be military. Wait, she is turning about. The name on the stern reads L-I-M-A-N."

Powell jumped up.

"Contact Cyprus Station and find out what kind of ship the Liman is, where she is supposed to be going and what flag she is she sailing under."

"No need. The Liman is a Russian Federation spy ship that was granted docking rights yesterday with an apparent medical emergency. I read the local Station report last night. The Russkies are claiming a crew member had a seizure of some sort and required immediate hospital treatment."

"And, you didn't tell me?"

"You had enough on your plate with Langley. If you remember, the original Liman sank after a collision in the Bosporus Straits. Intel says she was on route for an intelligence-gathering Op buzzing allied ships off the Syrian coast. With their main spy ship, the Viktor Leonov, cruising up and down the Eastern US coastline grabbing all the digital data she can from our bases there, Russia has had to rely on these smaller spy ships to cover the Mediterranean and the Syrian conflict."

"Fuck, Russian. You should have told me. Get the Cypriot Coast Guard on and tell them to stop that ship and check if Valentinova is at least leaving Cyprus of her own goddamned free will?"

"No chance. The Liman is a flagged Russian Federation ship. That would create a major diplomatic incident and we have had no time to lay the ground with the State Department or the locals. Let's face it, Valentinova is as good as back on Russian soil already."

"Jesus holy Christ. And your assessment is?"

"I don't think they would risk the Liman in a preplanned mission to snatch Valentinova, they would have used a lower-profile vessel, likely not even Russian flagged. No, I think she was on patrol nearby and they took advantage of that. It looks like the Russian Intelligence Services have picked up on our newspaper and cable news leaks and reacted quickly and decisively. They want Valentinova for conformation of the story and as a bargaining chip to use with Valentin, should he run or try and call in any political debts. Either way, Valentin and his wife appear to be well and truly fucked."

Powell turned to me, viciousness in his voice I had not heard before.

"Well Alexander, nice when a plan comes together. The General well and truly fucked up is what you wanted and genuinely fucked up is what you've got."

"*Mudak*, Asshole, deserves it."

No one disagreed with me on the trudge back down to the car.

*   *   *

It was Langley that had pushed for the last-minute pitch to Valentinova. Back in the car, now he had calmed down a little, already getting his story straight for the inquest back home, Powell double-checked my assessment that she wouldn't have cooperated anyway. I hadn't changed my mind.

"Besides, her departure for Russia is no big deal for us, we already have the information we need. But it is a different matter for her, I don't think she will have a pleasant trip home. Langley may be pissed their last-ditch plan failed, as such adventurism usually does, but it wasn't your plan. And besides, we can as easily use Valentinova's kidnapping itself as corroboration, right?"

"Go on."

"Leak whatever video footage, pictures and information you have of the abduction and the Liman's suspicious visit to Cyprus to local TV. Throw in the backstory that it has to do with Valentin's arrest for embezzlement back in Russia. Let the media people connect some dots and earn their pay. Once that hits the big US papers and they do their research, using their own sources, we will have the validation of our findings that Langley wanted."

"Not bad, not bad at all. It's almost like you have played these games before. I will make sure Langley know that it was your idea, I am in enough trouble already."

Powell laughed out loud.

When we got back to the hotel, he invited Stephen and I back to his suite, where the watchers were again setting up food on the balcony. This time there was a lot more beer and wine on the table and thankfully a few bottles of Stolichnaya.

"Well Langley's shit-show may have failed but our mission was a success. We nailed the money trail end to end, we have the proof, and in a couple of days the White House can respond to the Washington Post and New York Times questions about the fall of Valentin. Mission accomplished, as they say. At this point, it's traditional for us boys to have a wheels-up party. The surveillance teams are all heading back wherever they came from tomorrow."

Stephen headed outside to help.

"Take a seat Alexander. There is something I wanted to talk to you about."

Powell sounded serious.

"What?"

"Your future. You know you can't go back to Russia. It isn't safe."

I have to admit I had forced thoughts about what would happen after we got Valentin to the back of my mind. That was the only way I could operate. But now the question was posed I only one thing came to mind.

"I have to go back. It is my home and it is my duty."

"Duty? You think you have a duty to return and become another victim of the criminals responsible for the murders of Kislitsyn and Kirilov? They will never let you live. You are another loose end like Valentinova and like her they will see you as a traitor. They will not be merciful."

"Even so. It is home. Where else would I go?"

Powell thought for a moment.

"You lost your wife a few years ago?"

"Yes, I did, to lung cancer. It wasn't quick."

"I'm sorry to hear that. And you didn't have any children."

"We tried, there were, complications."

I could see where Powell was going but played along.

"You are an only child. You have no real family left in Russia."

Powell's file on me was, as usual, correct.

"I have no immediate family."

"So, nothing apart from your patriotic duty tying you to Russia, nothing familial, no deep personal relationships?"

"I suppose the answer to your question is no, but I have never really thought about it."

"I have to talk to Langley this evening as you know. I have ample ammunition to push back on any bullshit about what happened with their plan today. And I will not make light about your contribution to our successful mission."

"There is no need. I will get what I wanted. Valentin is done."

"Even so, an honorable mention in dispatches is called for. Tomorrow, with the departure of the surveillance teams, we are moving the Ops room to a safe house we have set up a few miles away. When we get there, we will have real-time contact with the watchers keeping an eye on Valentin until all the loose ends are tied up. I hope to have some news for you by then. In the meantime, get some rest. These wheels-up parties can get out of hand."

As I returned to my room to get some rest for a few hours I couldn't help wondering what news Powell could have for me.

27 PROPOSITION

October 6

The safe house was in the picturesque village of Zygi, on the southern coast, roughly halfway between the hotel where we ran the Ops center in Larnaca and where we had witnessed Valentinova's abduction in Limassol.

The front room, which is where Stephen had set up comms, had a bay window with a view of the small harbor below. It provided a colorful backdrop to the tedium of the live black and white pictures of the outside of Valentin's mansion. I borrowed his binoculars. Watching the boats come and go killed some time.

Powell hadn't appeared yet this morning. I guess he had a thick head from the bourbon and cigars at the party last night. Stephen and I were the ones tasked with liaising with the Moscow surveillance team keeping tabs on our main target.

It was slow going today. Valentin had broken his routine and not left the mansion for his usual commute to Yasenevo or the Kremlin. We both thought the change was significant and speculated that news of his wife's detention had reached the General. He could already know he was living on borrowed time. It was just after eleven when Powell showed up.

"Stephen, take a break."

He seemed more than happy to get his marching orders and go and get some fresh air. He hadn't moved for hours, where as I had spent the morning pacing up and down and sneaking off for cigarette breaks in the garden. By decree of both Agency men smoking was off limits in the house.

"I have spoken at length with Langley. In the end I called in a few favors and got my way. The Deputy Director is carrying the blame for missing out on Valentinova. Once I got the upper hand, I took advantage and discussed your contribution to this mission's success. We have a proposition."

"A proposition? What kind of a proposition?"

"A contract, of a sort."

"What would you want with an old, broken down, exiled but serving FSB officer? Well, I think I am technically still serving as they haven't yet told me I have been fired."

Powell produced an envelope from his coat pocket and handed it to me.

"Open it."

Inside was a Cypriot ID card in the familiar name of Anton Markevich with the same photograph of me they photoshopped for Scotland. There was a bankcard in that name too. I inspected the ID card closely.

"This is a very good forgery, my compliments to your technical boys."

"It's no forgery."

"What?"

"I have been a busy boy. I wasn't just up there nursing a hangover. I managed to persuade Langley to bid for this house in the name of a new company owned by young Mr. Anton Markevich there. These days anyone who invests more than five hundred thousand dollars in a business in Cyprus qualifies for a Cypriot ID card and Cypriot citizenship after just six months. We have a few friends with the local authorities so they expedited the back-dated application they received for Markevich."

"How convenient."

"Sure. Now you will find Mr. Markevich's company has been established as an independent anti-money laundering investigations consultancy. It has a contract with a company that is owned by a corporation, that is a subsidiary of a business, that may be owned outright by Langley. I am not sure exactly how many companies in the chain, or which has a contract with another, but you get my drift. Mr. Markevich's business receives a five thousand dollar a month retainer to maintain resource capacity and prioritize investigations on behalf of its owners and affiliates."

"Are you telling me the CIA is offering me a job?"

"Something like that. A contract anyway. But Langley keeps the house and wants five hundred dollars a month in rent."

"Are you serious?"

"Would I lie to you?"

"Yes, it's your job."

"But I don't lie to my own. These days we employ a lot of third-party consultants to do odd jobs for us. Some jobs we don't want on the books, some just don't justify the attention of our more, shall we say, valuable covert assets."

"I can't work for you. I am Russian. I can't work against Russian interests, even if I am against the crooks in charge just now."

"Other than this case, which you brought to us, we would never employ you to work on investigations directly involving Russian interests or assets. Or, for that matter, anything related to people you may know or have worked with. That is prudent and incidentally it is policy. But there are plenty of other things we need help with from time to time."

"Jesus, now I have heard everything."

"I am deadly serious. And to prove it go and check in the safe in the desk right there. The code is the last four digits of your FSB identification number. Something to remember them by."

Opening the desk, I typed the code in the small digital safe, the door clicking open on the last digit. Looking inside I could see my Makarov pistol. It seemed an eternity ago that Stephen had taken it, but it was just a few days. So much had happened.

"Thank you. This was my father's gun."

"And looks in fine working order, so it may have more than sentimental value. The contract we can offer you to think about is a monthly rolling contract. I thought that was best."

"Rolling contract? I don't understand the meaning of this?"

"It means it is a contract for one month at a time. So, you are free of contractual obligations at the end of each month, but if you do nothing the contract for the next month automatically kicks in. And if you want to go at any time after you have sorted out your plans for the future, you can go with my blessing and keep the Markevich identity into the bargain. My gift to you for your help with the whole Valentin sanctions thing."

I took my time to reply. Powell knew how to be patient when it suited his interests.

"That is a very interesting proposition, and absolutely and totally unexpected. I don't know what to say."

"You know how stubborn the bean counters in organizations like ours can be about authorizing additional expenditure, but I convinced them, so I sure as hell am not giving up on convincing you. You don't have to give me an answer now, but I want you to think seriously about it."

"Well, that's good, because I would not know what in the hell to say if you pushed me now."

"I know, it's a big decision, take your time."

He genuinely seemed keen on the idea. Then it dawned on me.

"If I take you up on your offer and ever got myself in trouble, I am not only deniable, but you could leak my FSB connections and blame whatever mess I have made on the Russians."

"The thought had occurred to me. It made my pitch to Langley easier to sell, I'll grant you. You are a more valuable asset because of it."

"And more expendable?"

He burst out laughing.

"That too. I know it is a lot to take in. Sleep on it tonight. In the meantime, let's see how Valentin plays it. Langley told me from our sources back in Moscow that your President and his friends were none too pleased about the additional sanctions we just announced. Putin was hopping mad and accepted several cabinet level resignations on the spot. Whether that is enough to satisfy the big money men behind him we will have to wait and see. But with those at the top who managed the scheme already fired, attention will doubtless shift to Valentin and the operational folks."

"Valentin didn't go into the office today."

"Stephen told me. We may not have that long to wait."

28 REVENGE

Stephen came back around one with lunch. I had to admit the local seafood was very good. I could get used to it, that was for sure, but I tried to put it out of my mind, along with Powell's offer, until the op was concluded. It wasn't so easy. With not much to do I found myself looking around the house and garden and planning what I would change if the place really was my own.

The two Americans were taking turns with the headset and responsibility for keeping in contact with Moscow. It was way below Powell's pay grade, but I got the distinct impression that despite what he said to the contrary, he really missed the field. All three of us at times crowded round the screen when it looked like something was happening, only to drift away after another false alarm.

All we had seen so far today was a guard stretching his legs every now and then. I counted six altogether outside the house. Two at the front gate, two walking the grounds and two taking a break in the makeshift guardhouse above the garage. They switched every two hours, like clockwork.

At five PM the guards switched again and Powell took the cue to hand the headset back to Stephen.

"Care for a walk Alexander?"

"Sure, I could do with some fresh air."

"I can't sit still for hours like I used to. We are getting old my friend."

"So true."

"If you think about the crazy stuff we did when we were younger. I could sit in an observation vehicle all day peeing into a bottle and not moving for hours on end."

"Once I had to hide in a loft listening in on a suspect for four hours straight. I can't even remember who the hell it was, or why we were spying on them, but I remember that stinking Moscow attic like it was yesterday. I have never been so cold in my life."

We made our way out of the French windows that led into the garden and through the gate to the narrow side street. Powell made small talk and avoided direct reference to the proposal he had made on behalf of the Agency. He was too smart to try and pressure me like that. He knew me well enough by now to know that such a direct approach would likely backfire. But he was not beyond mentioning how pretty the village and its surroundings were or how much he was enjoying the warm late summer weather. I have to admit I was thinking along the same lines myself.

Refreshed by the brisk sea breeze we returned to the

house through the manicured flowerbeds. Whoever had lived in the house before had been a keen gardener. That would be a challenge for me. I had not even kept a cactus alive in my old apartment. Damn, I had to stop this and focus on the operation.

Stephen heard us through the open windows.

"Come in, come in. We have activity. You are not going to believe this, but the guards have left Valentin's mansion. All of them, all together, just upped and went."

Powell rushed into the living room before me. I was as keen to see as him but when it came to it, I couldn't keep up with him. Entering, I could see the cameras on the front and back of the house showed no signs of life.

"What happened?"

"One of the guards on the front gate got a call on his cell phone. It looked a very brief conversation. Then he walked round to the back of the house and spoke to guards there, collected the two from the garage, and that was it. Within a few minutes a van with blacked out windows arrived and they drove off. Nobody checked in at the house from what we could see."

"They have been recalled."

"Looks like it."

"Alexander?"

"Those guards were hand-picked by Valentin himself and some of them have been with him for years. If someone recalled them, they must be very senior in the Russian Intelligence Services. And that they have been recalled at all is surely to get them out of the way so someone else can get at Valentin. I think whatever is going to happen is going to happen soon, perhaps a matter of hours."

"Stephen?"

"Makes sense. Grab your popcorn and take your seats gentleman, here comes the final act."

Then we saw him. Valentin appeared in the living room for the first time that day. The huge room had full-length floor to ceiling windows on two sides, open to the decks that caught the morning, afternoon and evening sun. We had a good camera angle on both aspects.

Valentin was still in a robe despite the hour. He seemed to be having an animated conversation on a cell phone, pacing up and down and waving his arms about. It wasn't one of the numbers we knew, none of the pop-ups for those were lit up on the monitor. He threw the phone down on a sofa and stomped off.

"He is heading toward the kitchen."

Just a minute or two later he returned with a bottle of wine and a glass. He stopped by the ostentatious stereo system next to the fireplace, picking up the remote, before pouring a large one and settling on an armchair facing the garden.

"What's he listening to?"

Stephen passed on Powell's question to the watchers, typing into the live messaging app, visible at the bottom of the screen. The reply came up almost instantaneously.

"Sounds like Tchaikovsky, the 1812. And it's very loud."

"How appropriate, Tchaikovsky's celebration of Russia's defense against Napoleon's Grande Armée. Valentin painting himself as the true patriot to the last."

"I bet that's the best Bordeaux in his collection. He is well known to my FSB colleagues as a keen collector of top-quality wine. If you wanted a particular posting, the best way to get Valentin's support was to give him a collectable French wine. He is rumored to have hundreds of bottles in his cellar, worth a small fortune."

"Well, apart from that one, I don't think he is going to have the opportunity to enjoy them."

Stephen spoke relaying a message.

"The guys are reporting someone entering the house after forcing the garage doors. He seems to be alone."

The silhouette of a person came into shot, emerging from the shadows behind the armchair. It almost looked like Valentin was expecting him and coward he was, he didn't want to look death in the face.

The figure raised an arm and the knife caught the light from the fireplace.

To my surprise Powell turned away from the screen. Perhaps he had just seen too much death over the years. I didn't blink. Valentin kicked his legs out wildly, then slumped at an odd angle over the side of the armchair breaking the wine glass and knocking over the bottle. I imagined blood running down his severed neck and mixing with the rich red wine on the polished wood floor. I felt nothing. The assassin waited, then moved quickly, checking a pulse as life ebbed away, then opening the side door to the deck and disappearing into the grounds behind the house.

"He was lucky it was quick and clean. Kislitsyn enjoyed no such mercy."

Powell had turned back to the screen.

"Well, that's that then."

That was that. Valentin was dead, my investigation was over. Suddenly I felt completely drained.

29 FUTURE

October 7

The rising sun sneaking in through the half open bedroom blinds woke me. From my bedroom window I could see the harbor and the few remaining fishing boats with their noisy seagull honor guard heading out for the days catch.

I was getting to know Powell better. Me getting this bedroom, the morning sun and the sea view were all part of his PSYOP campaign aimed at wearing down any resistance I could muster to his job offer. He knew they were the kind of things that at this stage of my life I would find hard to ignore.

And what did I have in Russia to go back to? With Kislitsyn and Kirilov gone I had lost my best friend and closest colleague. I had done my duty to them and kept going until the man responsible for their murders was dead. The untouchables at the top who planned the whole conspiracy and ordered the killings remained in power, ready to extract their revenge on me if I ever returned, perhaps even if I didn't.

I still missed Viktoriya, but I could just as painfully miss her from here, as from there. Every day hurt, wherever I was. And she would want me to stay here. She knew how much the failure of post-Communist Russia to cope with transition to a true democracy had hurt me. By then I had traveled the world and seen other countries, with working democracies. Back home, criminals stole the country's assets and then the country itself. The good people of the FSB who wanted to serve the country and the Russian people, ended up being little more than the hired muscle of the band of gangsters who had scrambled to the top.

Downstairs in the kitchen, I found Powell making a cooked breakfast. He even had been back to the little bakery in the village. I have always found the smell of fresh baked bread irresistible. Perhaps it was the peasant in me. This American was leaving no stone unturned.

"Good morning, Alexander."

"Good morning master chef. But this is too much. You are even employing the village bakery against me."

"I told you I wouldn't give up. How do you want your eggs?"

"Scrambled do you say, like you did before."

"Got it. I did plenty for both of us. Stephen was up early and has gone for one of his post operation wind-down epic runs."

Playing the housewife, I started to lay the table but Powell said it was warm enough to set the table outside, overlooking the pretty garden. He was relentless. I took a seat in the sunshine.

"Voila! Bradley Emerson Powell's signature scrambled eggs, Southern-style."

"Emerson?"

"After my granddaddy. A gentle giant of a man, but as tough a beat cop as you could ever wish not to meet."

"So, we are both from generations of law enforcement."

"We certainly are."

Powell set down the plates on the table. I was ravenous after my long uninterrupted peaceful sleep.

"Have you thought any more about my offer?"

"I am tempted, but what would it entail, day to day?"

"Hang on a minute and I'll show you. Eat your eggs before they get cold."

He seemed excited. I think he knew that he had broken my resistance. He disappeared into the house, and came back a minute later with a plain buff folder.

"Take a look at that."

I opened it with anticipation. The front page was a profile and identifying information for a Costas Orphanides, who looked a local, maybe in his mid-forties.

"He is your first assignment when you take the job. A Cypriot, he helped us with that Hezbollah operative here a few years ago. I don't know if you remember it, but he was in Cyprus targeting Israeli tourist hangouts in preparation for some sort of attack."

"I don't recall, sorry. What would you want me to do, were I to take you up on your offer?"

"Well, it seems he has gone and disappeared. Your job is to find him and let us know if he is ok and what he is up to. As yet, no sign of foul play and he may well have just run off with another woman or fled his bookmaker, for all we know. But we need to know and we need to make sure there is nothing for us to worry about."

"You could go to the Police?"

"Well, yes and no. As a last resort, maybe. But we would rather not highlight to the authorities here, or anyone else, that we have any interest in him."

I leafed through the remaining pages. A list of phone calls that covered the last three months and a press cutting from a local paper, with Orphanides named in a group photo of what looked like a wedding party.

"You find him and that takes care of your first month. If you have had enough after that we part ways with no hard feelings, as we discussed. At the very least you will get an all-expenses paid month long stay in beautiful Cyprus. What do you say?"

"I say ok, ok. I will give it a month and then let's see after that."

Powell looked a happy man to have landed his latest catch. He reached across the table offering his hand, which I took, the bargain sealed.

"Good man Alexander. I am sure you won't regret it."

And that was that. Out of the blue I was on the payroll of the CIA, the intelligence arm of the 'Main Enemy' that I had given decades of my life to battle. Only as an independent consultant though, I would argue if anyone questioned me. For me a new dawn, a new identity and a second chance.

EPILOGUE

November 10

In my first weeks as a CIA asset under non-official cover I had enjoyed myself. In particular, my two trips to Malta, an island I had not been to before.

Both had been to conduct financial investigations. Very routine, playing my money laundering investigator cover and dealing with local solicitors and bankers. Most of the information I wanted was public record, but was not available online. I picked up a little gossip too, mostly from getting the bankers a little drunk, over liquid lunches. I relayed it all to Langley.

It seemed like they were starting me off with some basic tasks, perhaps to settle me in, perhaps to test me out. It was no more than I had anticipated. Either way, I was happy living in a beautiful part of the world and working by myself. And the pay was good.

It was just over a month since Powell and Stephen had left me in the safe house. Guilt had gotten the better of me over time so I had discreetly organized a memorial service. Through one of my new friends in the village I organized it for St. Andrew's, the first church in Cyprus built in traditional Russian Orthodox style.

Rumor has it that the church had been entirely paid for by a resident Russian businessman. I don't know what his sins were, but they must have been great. The President of Cyprus attended the inauguration, perhaps to give thanks for the flood of Russian money, some of it possibly legal, which had saved his country from bankruptcy after the global banking crisis.

At the end of the service I went to a side altar to light candles for Kislitsyn and Kirilov. Lost in my private thoughts and memories, I would say not so much prayers, I didn't pay much attention to a large man on my right who had come to light his own candle. A second beefy figure approaching from the left put me on full alert. Would the Russian Intelligence Services really catch up with me here, of all places?

An undisguised Alabama accent layered over the Russian allayed my fears.

"*Privet tovarishch*, hello comrade."

"Powell, what the hell are you doing, trying to give me a heart attack?"

"I've come to pay my respects. I heard about the memorial service."

"Have you been spying on me?"

"I wouldn't stoop so low. I have just been monitoring the performance of a new contract employee. I am allowed to do that aren't I."

"I'll check the small print in my contract."

"Besides, I wanted to get your report first hand. What happened to Orphanides?"

"There was no great mystery in the end. He ran off to Greece with a neighbor's wife. Seems he had got her pregnant. He panicked and ran. Having spoken incognito to the wife, that was probably a wise move. Anyhow, now she has had the baby she has thrown him out and his wife won't take him back."

"Figures. Well, I guess he is available for work and he now probably has need of the cash."

With nothing more to report and beginning to feel uncomfortable in front of the altar I went to move away.

Powell grabbed my arm. He had a serious look on his face.

"Take a seat Alexander, I have some news for you and it is not good."

Powell motioned to a pew. I sat down without a word, numb, fearing the worst. Powell sat beside me, his bodyguard hovering somewhere behind us.

"Gerzkov is dead. They say he fell walking down the steps at his apartment building and hit his head, though there are no witnesses to be found. Elena too, she was hit by a supposedly drunk driver crossing the street after mass. According to the Moscow Police report anyway. She died in hospital later that night. The driver hasn't been identified. But Litvanov is safe at least, although he has retired. I guess he still has a few influential friends and maybe he kept a little something up his sleeve for a rainy day."

"My God, all dead? Kislitsyn, Kirilov, Gerzkov, poor Elena, all murdered. And for what?"

Powell spoke but I just didn't hear him.

"Sorry, what did you say?"

"I said, for the Russian Spymaster's legacy."

"What the fuck, Valentin's measly couple of million?"

"No Alexander, you misunderstand me. They all died for you and people like you. Kislitsyn was the spymaster and you, my friend, are his legacy."

I had no words. I wept.

*   *   *

ABOUT THE AUTHOR

Mark W. Doyle is a London-based former New York resident. Previously an Intelligence Analyst with UK Police and Counter-Terrorism he went on to work as a fraud and money laundering investigator for an international bank on both sides of the pond. Published work includes the non-fiction, 'AGENT ZEMLIAK: THE SPY WHO STAYED IN THE COLD' (2015), security and defense articles for a national US online news network (2014, 2015) and a national security article for INSS, the Israeli Institute for National Security Studies (2013). Mark is married to Kathy, a retired FBI Special Agent with 25 years of service.

Printed in Poland
by Amazon Fulfillment
Poland Sp. z o.o., Wrocław

66127507R00167